D1387268

ONE KICK

Michael Hardcastle was born in Huddersfield in Yorkshire, and after leaving school he served in the Royal Army Educational Corps in England, Kenya, and Mauritius. Later he worked for provincial daily newspapers in a variety of writing roles, from reporter and diarist to literary editor and chief feature writer. In 1988 he was awarded an MBE.

His first children's book was published in 1966 and *One Kick* is his ninety-first, but he still finds time to visit schools and colleges all over Britain to talk about books and writing. He now lives near Hull.

ff

ONE KICK

Michael Hardcastle

faber and faber

LONDON · BOSTON

First published in 1986
by Faber and Faber Limited
3 Queen Square London WC1N 3AU
This paperback edition first published 1989
Reprinted 1989 (twice)

Photoset and printed in Great Britain by
Cox & Wyman Ltd, Reading, Berkshire

British Library Cataloguing in Publication Data

Hardcastle, Michael
One kick.
1. Title
823'914[U]   PZ7
ISBN 0-571-15337-2

One

The coach wanted the free kick to be taken again. This time, he emphasized, players had to move, and move *fast*. They had to show determination to get to the ball and put the opposition under total pressure.

'Does he have to be a perfectionist *all* the time?' Steve muttered to Jamie. 'I mean, he just never gives us credit for getting anything right the first time, even when we do. It gets you down a bit, really.'

Jamie shrugged. 'That's just his style. You won't get him to change now. Anyway, he's done quite a good job for us, hasn't he? If Jonathan Fixby hadn't come to help us then Denholm Avengers would probably have vanished from the Sunday League by now.'

'I'm surprised you stick up for him the way you do,' said Steve, managing to look genuinely surprised. 'I think it's a bit much the way he's always getting at you, Jamie. He's not just stuck a knife into you – he keeps on twisting it.'

Before Jamie could make any reply Fixby himself was snapping his fingers at them like a crocodile exercising its jaws. It was a favourite gesture that could mean anything from 'Shut up!' to 'I'm not going to tell you again.' Hiding their reluctance with some effort, they took up their positions for the set piece. The kick was being taken from just outside the penalty area. An attacker was supposed to attach himself to the end of the defensive wall. Then, as the ball was flighted over it, the attacker was expected to nip behind the wall, meet the ball as it fell and flick it past the goalkeeper.

In theory, at least, the goalkeeper should have been coming out to catch it. Naturally, the success of the manoeuvre depended on near-perfect timing.

Denholm's centre-forward, Ian Pickering, was the player the coach had chosen to pull off this particular trick. He was tall, which was an advantage, but he wasn't the fastest mover in the team, and speed in execution was essential. As this was a training session, with the Avengers' defence taking on their own attackers, everyone knew what was going to happen – or *should* happen. The element of surprise, which would exist in a competitive match, was missing. Real pace was what, in Jamie's view, the centre-forward lacked. Ian went to the same school as Jamie and Steve and so all three played in the same team there, too. Because he could head the ball powerfully and shoot straight with either foot he scored plenty of goals. But, as Jamie saw it, many of those goals came from crosses which he himself supplied so accurately from the left wing. All the praise, though, was usually heaped on Ian's head, not his own.

Now, as the ball was struck, Ian moved tigerishly. Even though defenders knew what the ploy was he reached the falling ball ahead of everyone. Faithfully following instructions, the goalie raced from his line. He decided to

8

punch the ball clear. On this occasion all he managed to punch was the shoulder of a fellow defender who, unwisely, had got in his way. The pair of them exchanged mild insults, but the full-back hadn't really been hurt, so there wasn't much to complain about.

'That worked a treat,' Jonathan Fixby told them with obvious satisfaction. 'Well done. But we'll try it just once more before we pack up for the night. Only this time we'll use you, Jamie, as the striker. Got to keep our options open for the future, you know.'

Jamie couldn't conceal his astonishment. He'd always thought Fixby didn't really think of him as a striker in spite of the fact that he played in an attacking role. But he hurried to take up his position at the end of the new wall before the coach could change his mind. All the same, he couldn't help wondering about Jonathan Fixby's motive. Could it be that he was considering making changes in the Avengers' formation?

Once again the ball looped over invitingly. Jamie spun round to go after it. By now, however, defenders were tired of being outwitted. After all, the entire exercise seemed to be designed to show up their weaknesses. This time they weren't going to concede another goal. As Jamie broke away one of the full-backs tried a body-check while another deliberately attempted a trip. Both succeeded. Jamie bounced from one assault into another and inevitably finished up on the turf. The ball was snapped up by the grateful goalkeeper, who then punted it joyously away from the penalty area.

'If you do that in a match you'll give the other side a penalty kick, that's for sure,' Jonathan told the twin offen-

9

ders. 'So don't try that again, even in a training session. Right?'

The rebuke was so gentle that Jamie was dumbfounded. He could easily have suffered a bad injury, either in the contact or in the fall that followed. Yet Mr Fixby appeared not to have taken the slightest notice of his grievance. Shaking his head in disbelief, Jamie picked himself up and brushed loose earth from his left knee and thigh. Carefully he examined the area but it appeared the skin wasn't even grazed. His first instinct had been to retaliate, to hit out at the defenders who'd rammed him in the ribs. By now, though, both boys were out of range. He couldn't go charging after them and start a scrap over something that the coach himself clearly regarded as too trivial to mention.

'Well, I don't reckon you're any rival for my job as main striker,' remarked Ian Pickering, coming up to Jamie as the squad started to leave the training area. 'Honestly, the chance you had was much easier than the one I scored from. All that pace you're supposed to have didn't help there, did it?'

'But you saw what happened!' Jamie protested. 'I never had a chance! They just went straight into me – never even tried to get the ball. Deliberate obstruction *and* a foul – no, two fouls.'

Ian laughed. 'But that's what strikers have to put up with *all* the time, Jamie son. We have to learn to live with the bruises and the battle scars and all the little tricks the ref doesn't see, like the elbow in the ribs and the hand in your shorts. You just give the same treatment back when you get the chance. No good squealing about the sort of

10

things that go on in the box. Nobody wants to hear about that. Least of all guys like The Fixer. Results are all that count with him.'

There was no point in trying to argue with Ian Pickering, as Jamie had learned when they were at their previous school. Ian went serenely on his way, believing he knew all the answers. So far success had come easily to him on the sports fields, for he was a useful fast bowler and area champion in the high jump. He was not a misfit in the classroom, either, and it was his regular boast that he would become the youngest bank manager in the country. When anybody asked who cared about that sort of thing Ian had an instantaneous reply: 'You will! It's money that makes the world go round and bank managers control the supply.'

When they reached the dressing-rooms Jamie wondered whether Jonathan Fixby would say anything to him about the free kick fiasco; and, if he didn't, whether he should try to raise the matter with the coach. After all, Fixby was forever telling his squad that he preferred a 'full and frank discussion' on anything at all that was bothering them; silence and sullenness just made a bad situation worse.

He glanced at Steve, who was using the next peg. Steve was powerfully built, a midfielder with a good left foot. Usually he bubbled with enthusiasm, whether he was in the middle of a match or a training session. Yet tonight he seemed subdued, as if he had worries he couldn't share with anyone. Jamie regarded him as his closest friend, even though nowadays they really spent very little time together. Steve had an instinct for placing a pass and he'd

11

set up innumerable good openings for Jamie in matches for the school's second team and for the Avengers.

Jamie subsided on to the bench and began to pull on his trousers.

'What did you think about that last free kick?' he asked quietly.

Steve, who'd been on the point of walking over to the mirror to comb his thick black hair, paused.

'What about it?'

'Well, the way I was just completely clobbered when I went for the ball – you know, deliberately. And nobody said a word afterwards. Just ignored it.'

Steve shrugged. 'Not worth bothering about, Jamie. Just one of those things.'

'Yes, but – '

'Look, I said forget it. There's more important things to worry about than that. Training's over for another week, so let's get out of here. Trouble with you is, you don't let anything drop.'

Jamie was taken aback. Only a few minutes earlier, when they'd been on the field, it was Steve who had criticized Jonathan Fixby. Now, when Jamie had a point to make on the same subject, Steve apparently didn't want to talk about it.

He took his time putting on his socks and shoes, waiting for Steve to complete his grooming. No one else seemed inclined to chat about anything and Jonathan Fixby had disappeared. Jamie had half-expected the coach to come over and have a word about the next match, which was on Sunday against Dinthorpe, local and longstanding rivals. That was a game every Avenger, as well as their coach, was determined to win. League positions counted for little in such a match and therefore the fact that Dinthorpe were struggling this season couldn't be taken into consideration. They'd battle like mastodons to win that one. So, obviously, Fixby had nothing to say that couldn't wait until Sunday, when they all foregathered at the Dinthorpe ground half an hour before the kick-off.

'Going straight home?' Jamie inquired when Steve had finished admiring himself in the mirror.

'Got to. Promised my dad I'd give him a hand with the car, changing the tyres. He could do it just as well by himself but he thinks it's good for my soul to help.' Steve suddenly grinned. 'Got to keep in with him, though, because I want some money. And he's my only source. Unless you're feeling flush . . .'

'No chance!' Jamie replied quickly. As he knew from experience, lending cash to Steve could be a distinctly unprofitable business. He always had a good excuse for not repaying a loan on the promised date.

They made their way to the bus stop. As they waited, Jonathan Fixby swept past in his new Escort. He saw them and didn't stop, but he did give a sort of half-salute. Neither boy acknowledged it. They hadn't expected him to offer them a lift into town, but the hope had been there that he might. Jamie supposed that the coach could have been accused of favouritism if he had picked up one of the team. Fixby liked to describe himself as a democrat, and claimed that he treated everyone alike. Jamie, for one, wasn't sure that was true.

On the journey into town they didn't talk much, although Jamie wanted to discuss prospects for the Din-

13

thorpe match. Usually Steve was happy to speculate on the outcome of any game and the part they would play in the team's success. Now, shoulders hunched, his sports holdall clutched to his chest by folded arms, he muttered only that he was thinking: thinking of ways to raise some cash quickly. That was the priority of the week. It was one that excluded conversations about soccer.

When they parted at the bus station Steve headed straight for the cafeteria: he claimed he could never think properly on an empty stomach.

Jamie got home sooner than he expected. Clive Forman, the Austerbys' next door neighbour, was at the bus station with his car to pick up his wife, who had been on a shopping trip by coach to London. Jamie accepted their offer of a lift with alacrity, but they didn't have much to say to him (clearly it wasn't his night for friendly chats). After a perfunctory inquiry about whether he'd enjoyed his football they talked non-stop to each other about London prices, crowds, traffic fumes and the weather in Oxford Street, London, and High Street, Denholm – identical, apparently, to the Formans' amazement. It was a thoroughly boring ride home, in Jamie's opinion, but it was better than waiting for another bus. He thanked them with excessive politeness when they dropped him off. They were really very tolerant about the number of times he and his sister went to retrieve the various footballs, tennis balls, cricket balls and other projectiles they managed to send on to the Formans' land.

Vicky ambushed him as he passed through the gap between two beech hedges. She'd hidden herself behind the trunk of a plum tree and sprang out when he entered their garden. He wasn't a bit surprised to see that she was wielding a hockey stick.

'I *knew* you'd get a lift from Mr Forman,' she greeted him.

'You know more than I did.'

'Well, I saw him about to set off to pick up Mrs F., so I told him he'd probably meet you because you'd be getting back from your training session about the same time,' she said at tremendous speed. 'I wanted you to get here quick so that I can demonstrate my new dribbling technique.'

She paused and then rushed on: 'Actually, I want to see if you can take the ball off me when I'm in top gear.'

'Vicky, it's practically pitch black already – and I've got some maths homework to do. I can't put it off another night.'

He knew that would be a feeble excuse, because she didn't recognize the need to do homework at any time. She was almost two years younger than he and so hadn't been burdened with it yet. Whenever the subject was mentioned she treated it as just an annoying interruption to the seemingly endless delights of her day. Which, Jamie always agreed, homework was for everybody.

The intensity of the pleading in her grey eyes won him over, as it usually did. He knew he was lucky to have a sister he liked so much (and who adored him), one who was almost as obsessed by sport as he was. People meeting her for the first time, and taking note of what their mother called her 'urchin cut' hairstyle, invariably referred to her as a tomboy. Vicky didn't mind a bit.

'Just five minutes then, not a second longer,' he ruled.

15

The Austerby family had a large garden, at the end of which was what Mrs Austerby rather grandly called The Orchard; but then, it did contain several apple trees and plum trees. There was no objection to the children using the grassed areas in between the trees as a sports arena. Both of them regarded the trees as stationary defenders around whom they could dribble a football or hockey ball or tennis ball whenever they wanted to practise new moves. But they had to move out of The Orchard when they switched to cricket and tennis.

Vicky's passion was hockey. Like her brother, she was built more on the lines of a greyhound than a bulldog, but her speed and stick skills kept her out of the tougher encounters of the game on most occasions. In any case, she was stronger than she looked and regularly played in goal in soccer games between the local boys; even more impressively, she stood up uncompromisingly to fast bowlers as a batsman. With no thought for her own safety, she would dive at the feet of onrushing forwards to snatch up the ball and save her side. If she got a knock then she concealed the pain or shrugged it off as not worth worrying about. In that sense, she was more resilient than her brother.

She had brought out a white golf ball in place of the usual hockey ball because it was harder to manoeuvre and easier to see. In anticipation of Jamie's support, she'd also brought a stick for him.

He didn't stand much chance against her. Her close control was exceptional, the result of hours of practice on her own in the past week. Switching her stick from right to left and back again, she dribbled the ball past him, and the immobile fruit trees, almost at will. Plainly she was in exhilarating form.

'Come on, Jamie, you're not trying to tackle me,' she complained.

'I am, I am,' he answered, and lunged at player and ball to demonstrate keenness. He missed the player but stood awkwardly on the ball.

Pain flared through his ankle. His gasp as he sank to the ground to nurse the injury seemed to Vicky to be as loud as an alarm bell.

'Oh, Jamie, I'm sorry, *really* sorry.' She was on her knees, putting her arms round his shoulders. 'Honestly, I didn't think I touched you.'

'You didn't,' he assured her through clenched teeth. 'Like an idiot, I stood on the ball. Think I must have sprained it – my ankle, I mean.'

'Do you want to try and walk a bit, see if it holds you up all right?' Vicky asked anxiously.

'Give it a moment,' he said, breathing heavily and then biting his lip.

'Look, think of something cheerful – something terrifically exciting like – like having a double helping of Christmas pud; or – or getting a Cup Final ticket and meeting all your favourite players in the dressing-rooms at Wembley. That'll help to take the pain away, I'm sure it will.'

All Jamie could think of at that moment was whether he'd be fit enough to play for Denholm Avengers in the match against Dinthorpe on Sunday morning.

Two

Jamie had been awake for about five minutes and was still thinking about getting up when Vicky burst into his room. Her first move was to cross to the window and sweep the curtains aside.

'Right, now I've thrown some light on the scene, what's the vital news?' she demanded.

'What – what're you talking about, Vicky?' He was still a bit drowsy.

'The *ankle*, of course! What else is so vital to your sporting career at present, stoo-pid?'

'Oh, that. Well, I don't know yet, do I? I mean, I haven't tested it.'

'Well, come on then, what're you waiting for, Jamie? Get on your feet and test it. Come ON!'

Without even giving him time to make a move she darted forward and yanked the duvet from his bed.

'Hey, cut that out!' he protested, hastily trying to cover himself up. 'We may be brother and sister but I'm entitled to privacy in my own bedroom. Especially my own bed!'

'Oh, don't be so stuffy,' she told him with the mocking grin that she always produced when she was in this sort of mood. 'I know all about boys and you're no different from

18

the rest from what I can see. Now, get a move on, Jamie!'

He was in no position to argue with her. For it was perfectly true that she spent most of her free time in the company of boys and shared in their sporting activities. In her experience, as she'd declared several times, most girls were either 'too soft' or 'boring' or both.

Reluctantly, he swung his legs off the bed and then, very tentatively, tried a couple of steps. None of the pain he'd experienced in the past few days since the accident. Not a twinge of any description. Before committing himself, however, he took another, firmer, step and tested extra weight on the injured left ankle.

'Oh, come on, stop dramatizing everything,' Vicky ordered with more than a hint of exasperation. 'What's the verdict?'

'It – seems – not – *too* – bad,' he admitted eventually. 'Yes, not too bad. Maybe I'll survive to play again after all.'

'If you can start making feeble jokes like that then you must be feeling pretty good, to say *the least*,' she told him. 'Remember, I *know* you. Look, do you want me to take the strapping off for you? Must be tricky doing it for yourself.'

'No, no,' he replied hurriedly. 'I can do that later. Might as well leave it on until I leave for the match. Give it all the support I can.'

'Well, all right then,' she said disappointedly. 'Look, if you don't take simply *ages* to get dressed I'll have some scrambled eggs and bacon ready for you. You need some good food inside you on a morning like this. So get your skates on, brother.'

As she departed for the kitchen he went over to the window to see for himself what sort of day it was. The sight of ice on the garden pond and a light scattering of snow on the lawn and paths surprised him. He hadn't realized the night had been so cold. The pitch, of course, would be rock hard. That would be a great disadvantage following the kind of injury he'd suffered but there was nothing he could do about it. The great thing was that the ankle seemed to be as good as ever. Plainly the ice treatment he'd given it immediately after the accident had paid off. He'd strapped it up as a further precaution, on Vicky's advice, and that, too, must have helped his recovery.

Now that he was confident he'd be fit enough to play, he thought about the match against Dinthorpe as he dressed. They had a reputation as a very physical side, one always prepared to achieve by force what they might not be able to achieve by skill. On a couple of occasions that season they'd had two players sent off in the same match. Even so, their results had been good enough to keep them just above Denholm Avengers in the League table. Today, as Jamie knew, they'd be determined to widen that gap, not only because neighbourhood prestige was at stake but to give themselves a chance of challenging for the championship of the Division. In every respect, it would be a tough game.

In the bathroom and as he passed his parents' bedroom he was as quiet as possible. They cherished their Sunday lie-in and so he and Vicky had vowed never to disturb them except in an emergency. They were always supportive of their children's sporting activities but they couldn't be expected to turn out on a chilly Sunday morning for anything less than a Cup Final! Jamie and Vicky generally got their own breakfasts on Sunday, but as Jamie had a match ahead of him Vicky was prepared to cook for them both today.

'I presume you'll score a fantastic hat-trick this morning to give a happy ending to the story of the return of the wounded warrior,' she remarked as she handed him a plate of beautifully yellow eggs and marginally scorched bacon.

'*If* I get the chance. No guarantee I'll even be in the side today, is there?'

'What! You mean all my brilliant work in getting you fit again could be wasted because they don't pick you for the team? They wouldn't do that to you, would they, Jamie?'

He shrugged and chewed on a section of bacon before answering. 'Well, he's a funny guy is Fixby, our coach. He says nobody, but *nobody*, is a fixture in *his* teams. I don't believe that, actually, because I bet he'd never drop Ian Pickering for a start. Thinks Pickers is a genius or something. Which he's not, not by a long way. Anyway, Fixby says everyone's got to *earn* his place. And as he doesn't seem to have the highest possible opinion of me at the moment anything could happen. I could be dropped, just like that.'

Jamie didn't totally believe all that but it sounded like a thoughtful evaluation of the situation – as well as common sense. If he were dropped, though, he knew he'd feel devastated.

'Anyway, what about you, Vick?' he inquired, not only out of politeness. 'Are you going to play hockey and clobber somebody on the ankle? You'll certainly know how to treat the wound if you do.'

'Hey, that's a bit below the belt!'

She looked quite wounded by the remark.

'Well, that's me getting my own back, then, for you dragging the bedclothes off me,' he grinned. 'That was definitely ungentlemanly conduct and any decent referee would have sent you off for that offence.'

'Don't kid yourself,' she said quite fiercely and went off to her bedroom to change, leaving him to do the washing-up.

There was a distinct nip in the air when he left the house and although the sun had appeared it was the colour of a pale lemon. It was definitely a day for rubber-soled boots. The real worry, though, was whether the referee would allow the match to begin.

In fact, the official was making up his mind on that sub-ject when Jamie arrived at the pretty, tree-lined ground on the edge of the town. Purposefully, he marched across it in one direction and then re-crossed it along the other diag-onal. In the goal areas he paused and squatted down to peer with evident suspicion at the texture of the turf, or as much of it as he could see. Now and again, he prodded it with a forefinger.

'You know, I think he's trying to decide whether to *taste* it, see what sort of flavour it has,' Jonathan Fixby mut-tered.

The three Denholm players who'd arrived ahead of Jamie laughed in unison. It wasn't within howling distance of a joke but it wasn't sensible not to appreciate the coach's sense of humour. Nothing had been said about the composition of the team and Jamie supposed Mr Fixby wouldn't announce it until he knew whether the game was on. As usual, the coach was wearing his ancient donkey jacket and the black-and-white scarf that was in complete contrast to the pale blue shirts and shorts of the Avengers' official strip. Someone had once asked him why he sported another team's colours but he refused to answer. Popular opinion was that the scarf had been given to him in his own playing days by an old girl-friend for whom he still yearned: so if she ever turned up at one of their matches and saw what he was wearing she would be bound to fall into his arms again to reward him for his undying loyalty.

Impressively, the Dinthorpe squad arrived in their own minibus, on each side of which in red lettering ran the legend: Dinthorpe are Dynamite! Without turning their heads, the Avengers glanced at their opponents as they piled out of the vehicle. As everyone knew, they were a solid-looking bunch; three of them were even taller and heftier than Ian Pickering, Denholm's gangling striker.

After jumping up and down on the spot to ease cramped limbs they moved off to the opposite side of the pitch and watched the referee continue his solemn ritual. No one said a word. The last thing anybody wanted to do was to antagonize the official and cause him to call the game off. Dinthorpe believed they were in the middle of a winning streak and the thought of a week's interruption horrified them.

More Avengers turned up and grouped themselves around Jonathan Fixby. Among them was Guy Kelton, a frail-looking boy who had played in the first team only once. Jamie was surprised to see him there. He hadn't known that Guy was included in the squad for this match. Young Kelton hardly had the physique to withstand the attention of Dinthorpe defenders.

'What the heck does the ref think he's doing now, Boss?' Ian Pickering asked as the man started to jump up and down in various spots, making sure each time that he landed on his heels.

Fixby shook his head in wonderment. 'Your guess is as good as mine, Ian. I reckon he's just a bit of a show-off whenever he has a captive audience.'

'Perhaps he's just cracked, like the ice!' Jamie joked.

When the rest of the players noticed that the coach smiled they followed suit.

That test, however, seemed to have proved decisive, for moments later the referee came off the pitch and approached Mr Fixby.

'It's treacherous in places but I've decided we can go ahead with the game,' he announced. 'But, first, there are one or two areas that need to be sanded. I presume there *is* sand available?'

'Oh yes, there's a pile of the stuff behind the pavilion.'

'Good. Then perhaps you'd organize some of your players to spread it over the worst-affected areas in the goal-mouths and the centre circle. The groundsman doesn't appear to have troubled to turn up this morning.' He sighed theatrically. 'Doesn't make my work any easier, you know, having to cope with *everything* myself.'

Guy and Jamie were the ones ordered to carry out the sanding operation, with the aid of a couple of shovels borrowed from the farmhouse on the far side of the ground.

'Didn't realize you were in the squad for this match,' Jamie remarked to Guy as they hurried through their tedious task. 'Do you think you'll be playing?'

'Mr Fixby phoned me up last night. Said he'd been listening to the weather forecasts and it was going to be a hard pitch today. So he wanted someone fast and nippy on the wing.'

Jamie's heart sank. That was almost how the coach might have described his own style of play. So if Fixby wanted a similar kind of player then it was obvious he didn't have much confidence in Jamie. Unless, of course, he intended to play both of them, one on either wing. . . . His hopes rose again. Yes, that was a likely tactic.

'Sounds as though you'll be in the team, then,' he said to Guy.

'Hope so. But he didn't promise anything.'

By the time they got to the changing-room the coach was already launched on his tactical talk. He barely glanced at them as they quickly stripped off. It was the team habit to put their shirts on last and so the freshly-laundered pile was still on the bench beside the coach, untouched. When he was in a particularly jaunty mood Fixby himself picked the shirts off one by one and flung them to the chosen eleven.

'I want to win this one, so *you* want to win this one,' he concluded. 'We don't want a team like Dinthorpe crowing over us. Local prestige is at stake here as well as League points. There's no reason on this earth why we shouldn't defeat them so long as you lot all play up to your best form. So don't let them knock you off your stride. Keep the ball tight and give nothing away. Remember, they might have the muscle but we've got the skills. Any questions?'

Jonathan Fixby always claimed that he welcomed questions at any time, that anyone else's opinion was as valuable as his own. That attitude helped to make him the democrat he insisted he was. But the players rarely tested him on that score. They simply didn't believe him. Moreover, most of them just wanted to be told what to do. So, now, heads went down and players stared woodenly at the floor, waiting to be released from the minor embarrassment of being invited to contribute to a tactical discussion when all they wanted to do was to go out on to the pitch and play in the way they always played.

'OK, then,' he resumed after an interval of a few seconds, 'here's the line-up. I've made just the one change from the last match. I'm putting you, Guy, on the left wing in place of Jamie. I want you to use your ball control, keep the ball as much as you can and *torment* 'em. On a slippery surface you'll have the advantage of them because it's less easy for big defenders to turn and twist. So be prepared to take them on every time, Guy, in one-to-one situations. Hold the ball and taunt them. When I want you to start crossing it into the middle, aiming for Ian's big nut, I'll pass the word.'

The coach paused and then added: 'Jamie, son, I'm giving you the sub's job. In these conditions the likelihood is you'll get on to the pitch at some stage of the game. So put your tracksuit back on and keep me company on the bench. Right, boys, put your shirts on and let's get out there and drill holes through the other lot.'

The first thought in Jamie's mind as he pulled on the No. 12 shirt was to wish that he'd never said anything to Vicky about there being no guarantee he'd be in the team today. Fate had been tempted and it had played him a rotten trick. He was convinced that his ball-playing skills were at least the equal of Guy's: and certainly he was a better, and stronger, all-round player. Guy wasn't the sort of attacker to go straight for goal when the need arose. Well, he'd told Vicky he might be dropped: and dropped he was. He felt physically sick.

There wasn't a bench for anyone to sit on, and that suited Jamie. He didn't want to be in close proximity to the coach and have to talk to him all through the match. Not for one moment did he believe that Fixby had any intention of putting him on at any stage. The coach didn't care for making substitutions unless they were really forced upon him because of injuries.

Jamie decided he would keep warm by sprinting up and down the touchline at regular intervals. In addition, that would remind Fixby of his presence and his fitness. Such activity might even encourage the Avengers on the pitch to keep playing at their best to avoid the risk of being substituted. But then, he realized, if the team played *too* well he himself would not get back into the side very quickly. So he decided to ration his sprints after all.

In their red-and-black striped shirts and black shorts Dinthorpe looked an even more formidable outfit than when they'd climbed from the minibus. Power seemed to be packed into every bulging muscle in necks and thighs and calves. In the shooting-in before the referee called the skippers to the centre the shots which went past the goalie threatened to rip the netting from the stanchions.

By now a score or more of supporters had drifted into the ground and several stationed themselves behind the Denholm goal after the toss-up and choosing of ends; clearly they expected to enjoy an avalanche of goals at close range. Stuart Elcro, Avengers' goalkeeper, understandably appeared rather discomfited by some of the remarks the spectators were making about his competence, or lack of it, and the suffering he was sure to undergo in the next ninety minutes. Stuart, though, had been told often enough by Jonathan Fixby that only those goalkeepers who learned to shut their ears to stupid taunts and general abuse reached the top class. And Stuart possessed a fierce determination to play one day for his country.

Initially, the action was all at the other end. From the kick-off Ian Pickering swung the ball out to the left flank. Guy Kelton collected it, exchanged a neat one-two with Steve Derome who was backing up as instructed, and then ran at the defence. Dinthorpe's towering right-back automatically started to back-pedal and seconds later was flat on his back. On one of the slippier patches of frozen turf he'd been unable to save himself when he felt his feet sliding in different directions.

Guy rounded him nonchalantly. With Ian Pickering charging towards the far post it was the moment to sling in a cross for a heading opportunity. Instead, the chance was wasted because Guy was intent on mesmerizing another defender.

The slim, fair-haired winger turned his next opponent first one way, then another, before trying to nutmeg him by pushing the ball between the player's legs and then nipping round him. But there his progress ended, because the ball cannoned off the Dinthorpe defender's ankle and over the by-line for a corner.

'Great start, boy, great start!' Jonathan Fixby yelled at the top of his voice as his team surged forward for the corner-kick.

Apart from the fact they hadn't managed to score a goal yet it was exactly the opening salvo he wanted. If Dinthorpe took the initiative they would be very hard to overcome. Fixby believed his own team possessed talent but not necessarily the temperament to complement it. Some of his players soon became dispirited if the game was going against them. He glanced along the touchline to where Jamie was running gently on the spot. He liked the boy but thought he needed toughening up.

Dinthorpe's goalkeeper had to produce an acrobatic save to keep out a downward header from Ian Pickering. From the corner-kick the ball swerved awkwardly in the fretful wind that had sprung up and both central defenders missed making contact. Ian, as was his fortunate habit, was in the right spot at the right moment to send in the header. Until the goalie's fingertips turned the ball aside close to the post Ian was convinced he'd scored. His arms were already shooting skywards in a salute to his own achievement.

Nothing went right for Dinthorpe in the opening minutes. On the one occasion when their own centre-forward went clear with the ball he stumbled over a divot and lost the ball when no opponent was within metres of him.

Moments later a defender handled accidentally on the edge of the penalty area and from the free kick Steve Derome drove a whiplash shot against the left-hand post.

Despite a brave dive by the goalkeeper into the cluster of legs trying to make contact with the ricochet he couldn't get his hands on the ball. It spun away again from someone's knee and Ian Pickering was in precisely the right spot to stab the ball into the net by the far post.

Against all the predictions, and in the midst of a volley of jibes from the Dinthorpe fans, Denholm Avengers had taken the lead. What's more, that goal had come before Dinthorpe had sent in even one shot for Stuart Elcro to save or watch sail harmlessly past his net. The cascade of congratulations that descended on the goal-scorer continued until the entire team was back in its own half and awaiting the whistle for Dinthorpe to kick off again.

No one appeared more elated than Jonathan Fixby. He was, literally, dancing along the touchline, his hands above his head, clapping loudly and rhythmically. Jamie was astonished. His own yells of glee seemed hollow in comparison. He'd never seen the coach celebrate in this style; but then, he realized, he rarely had time to observe Fixby's reactions because he himself was usually on the pitch when a goal was scored.

It was as inevitable as night following day that Dinthorpe would strive to equalize at the earliest opportunity – and that they'd launch an all-out assault to create that opening. Like every other coach in the game, Fixby was regularly warning his players not to relax for a split second after scoring a goal. Every team was at risk from a counter-punch at that moment. So players had to steel themselves to withstand it – or lose the advantage they'd just gained. In the euphoria of taking the lead midfielders, in particular, became temporarily careless, most probably because they'd contributed significantly to the build-up to the goal but hadn't been credited with the glory.

So, it wasn't altogether surprising that, when Dinthorpe drove forward again, the clumsy tackle that upended their striker and halted the attack was committed by Steve Derome. While the victim received prolonged treatment on the pitch from his manager Steve was given a stern warning by the referee. At one point it looked as though the ref's hand was straying towards his notebook pocket: but Steve survived with a verbal caution instead of a booking. He made a point of going across to the Dinthorpe striker to offer an apology, but was waved away by the aggrieved manager. For a while it seemed as though the injured player was going to be taken off for still more patching-up but, in the end, he stayed to hobble about as the free kick was taken. By now, of course, the Dinthorpe fan club was howling for the blood of an Avenger.

The kick came to naught, the attack petered out and once again play swept back to the other end. Guy came infield briefly to collect a loose ball and then take on his usual adversary. The Dinthorpe full-back was beginning to display his resentment of the treatment he was getting from the little winger. Twice within two minutes he barged into him as he went for the ball. On neither occasion did it look to be a real foul and the referee took no action. In any case, Guy gave no sign that he was even thinking of retaliating. Because of his size he was used to being pushed around: when, that is, defenders caught up with him.

Dinthorpe seemed incapable of stringing two decent passes together and their isolated attacks were breaking down even before they reached the edge of Denholm's penalty area. Their biggest problem was their inability to judge the bounce of the ball on the hard surface.

Once, towards the end of the first half, Jonathan Fixby had to race on to the pitch to attend to John Blakiston, his central defender, who'd suffered in a crash of heads with a Dinthorpe striker. At first, it looked like a serious knock and Jamie began to think he'd be called on as substitute after all. If that happened then Ian Pickering, because of his height, would be drafted into the back four as an emergency defender: and Jamie would probably be told to take Ian's place as centre-forward. He tried to convince himself that he wanted John to be restored to instant good health; but he knew that if he wasn't then the move to centre-forward would suit him perfectly.

But, shaking his head woefully after being doused with cold water several times, John recovered and Jamie kept his tracksuit on. So far Jonathan Fixby hadn't spoken a word to him during the match and Jamie decided it might be wise to stay closer to the coach and offer a comment of his own now and again. It was just possible Mr Fixby thought he was sulking because he'd been dropped.

'Looked a nasty knock that, Boss,' Jamie remarked as the coach returned with his medical bag.

Fixby shrugged. 'Nothing worse than usual. John's a tough lad. Very tough. The odd bang on the head doesn't worry him so long as he can see straight.'

Jamie tried not to interpret that remark as any implied criticism of his own attitude whenever he was kicked or elbowed or trodden on. The coach's expression didn't give any clues to what he was really thinking. Indeed, his attention switched to the forwards and the very positive run that Ian Pickering was making into the Dinthorpe penalty area. He was only just inside the box when, trying to evade a tackle, he lost the ball and fell over.

The referee didn't hesitate in blowing his whistle and pointing to the penalty spot.

He'd anticipated protests, and he got them: protests that were loud and long and legitimate, even in the eyes of some of the Denholm players. Ian Pickering actually looked quite embarrassed by the decision, though that hadn't prevented his picking up the ball in case any opponent had the foolish idea of hoofing it out of the ground to demonstrate his displeasure. He knew he'd stumbled and wasn't the victim of a foul. But that was the luck of the game: many times he'd pleaded for a penalty when it was obvious to everyone that it should be awarded and yet the ref wouldn't listen. So this kick would simply make up for one of those dreadful errors of judgement.

John Blakiston stepped up to place the ball on the spot but then had to wait until the referee silenced the most vociferous protester by booking him. Jamie had his fingers crossed that John's eyesight was as good as ever. It seemed to be. For he hit the ball hard and true and it went into the net close to the angle of the left-hand upright and the crossbar. Certainly Dinthorpe's goalie hadn't a hope of reaching it.

So, against all predictions, the Avengers led 2–0 with two minutes to go to half-time.

The fury of Dinthorpe was bound to be unleashed now

33

and Jonathan Fixby was signalling from the touchline like a pianist working on a slow movement. 'Keep calm, keep calm,' he was calling. The worst thing now, in his eyes, would be if his players in their excitement let Dinthorpe back into the game by conceding a soft goal. The Avengers had only to keep their heads to win this match, as he saw it.

At the moment there wasn't enough discipline among the Dinthorpe players for them to be able to play constructively. Still incensed by the penalty award, some were kicking anywhere and almost anything. Somebody was bound to suffer soon. And the one who did was Guy Kelton. His over-elaborate approach play down the wing, and his taunting turns, predictably further enraged the full-back. Guy was scythed to the ground.

This time the notebook was in the ref's hand before he signalled to the offender that he wanted him. He was lucky, in Jamie's view, not to be sent off. The foul was plainly intentional. Guy had to be lifted to the touchline and Jamie went across to help. The pain-killing spray came out and Guy's left knee got the treatment. But the boy seemed more winded than in pain, though he would surely have bruises to show by the end of the day.

'There's less than a minute to go, so I'll keep you off until the interval,' Fixby told him. 'You should be right enough after that to take 'em on again, son. OK?'

Guy, leaning back on his hands on the turf, socks rolled down to his slender ankles, just nodded. Jamie's hopes went down again. The boss wasn't going to change a winning team, and that's what the Avengers looked like.

Fixby told his players exactly that at the interval. They

only had to keep their heads to win; they must push the ball around and retain possession; attack whenever possible because another goal would definitely seal it; above all, do nothing rash.

Dinthorpe's manager was equally talkative and he was still issuing instructions when his players returned to the pitch. Their scowls underlined determination to get back into the game.

Within a couple of minutes of the resumption Dinthorpe, in a well-organized thrust through the centre, launched a strong attack on the Denholm goal. A fiercely-hit shot from just inside the box brought an absolutely brilliant save by Stuart Elcro. It was all the more impressive because he'd had so little to do for so long. He flung himself sideways to push the ball away and then, when it bounced back from the inside of the post, he somehow managed to gather it in both arms as he rolled over and over.

'Stupendous, stupendous!' exclaimed Jonathan Fixby. And so it was. It also seemed to deflate most of the Dinthorpe players. They sensed, now, it wasn't to be their day. Moments later Guy Kelton was cutting in from the left and letting go with a strong shot of his own that very nearly brought the Avengers their third goal, Jamie was impressed. He hadn't suspected that Guy would take the initiative in that way. Clearly his confidence hadn't been affected by the bad tackle on him just before half-time.

What had changed, though, was the formation at the back for Dinthorpe. The full-backs had switched places so that the one who'd been booked for his tackle on Guy was now operating on the other wing. Quite undeterred by that, Guy was soon tormenting his new opponent and endeavouring to evade lunging attempts to dispossess him.

'Pretty soon, they'll lean on him too hard again and then we'll pick up another free kick in a vital position,' remarked Jonathan Fixby as he and Jamie stood side by side for once. 'If they're really crude and careless we might even get another penalty. Then all my plans will have worked out.'

Jamie was quite staggered by the coach's cunning approach to team selection and his use of people to get what he wanted. Now he couldn't help wondering exactly how Fixby regarded his (Jamie's) role in the squad. It was hateful to think that he might be regarded as little more than a puppet.

Sure enough, Guy soon went down after another clattering tackle and this time he limped heavily after treatment. Nothing came of the free kick from the edge of the box and the defender who'd put Guy down received only a finger-wagging rebuke.

'Get stripped off,' the coach ordered Jamie as he returned to the touchline after attending to Guy. 'And warm up fast. I'll give Guy another minute to see if he improves but I doubt he will.'

Jamie did as he was told. He tried not to look too pleased, for he was conscious that he was only replacing an injured player. In exactly the time he'd forecast Fixby signalled he wanted to make the substitution. Guy could only hobble when the ball moved in his direction and there was no point at all in keeping him on the pitch. He had pain in his eyes as he touched hands with Jamie to wish him luck.

'Just play the same role as Guy,' was the final instruction. 'But you can go for goal if there's a real opening.'

Within seconds, he was in the action. Steve Derome, eager to restore their partnership, threaded a pass to him between two opposing midfielders. Jamie had hardly set off with the ball, however, when Dinthorpe's 'new' right-back barged into him and 'accidentally' trod on Jamie's ankle as he got to his feet. Because the defender had his body between the incident and the referee the latter didn't see the offence. Jamie certainly felt it. Had it been the ankle injured in the hockey practice he was sure he wouldn't have been able to stand. He recognized that the full-back was deliberately leaving his mark to indicate that he intended to come out on top in every encounter they had. Jamie was now determined to prove that it would be otherwise. He knew that Guy had impressed Jonathan Fixby; so he must do at least as well.

Dinthorpe were becoming increasingly desperate to score and so get back into the game with a chance of picking up points. Nothing, though, was going right for them and frenzied appeals for a penalty when they claimed John Blakiston had handled the ball in the box were curtly rejected. It was John himself, moments later, who belted the ball up towards the halfway line, midway between the centre circle and the left-hand touchline.

Jamie dashed for the ball, intending to head it on to put Ian Pickering clear for a run at goal. His marker, the full-back, was almost literally on his heels as Jamie jumped for the header. And when Jamie came down, the full-back landed on top of him. Once again his boot found Jamie's ankle.

The pain was excruciating. But the fierceness of it only

matched the fierceness of his anger. Unhesitatingly, he got to his feet and, with his right foot, lashed out at the full-back, who himself hadn't regained his balance at that moment.

Jamie and the full-back weren't the only ones who heard the sound of a bone break.

Three

Jonathan Fixby was among the first to react. He was racing on to the field with his medical kit almost before the full-back collapsed. At that moment the coach really had no idea which player had suffered more in that dreadful clash. His aim, though, was to give Jamie whatever comfort and protection he could.

Jamie stared, aghast, at the inert form of his opponent. Every hint of colour had suddenly vanished from the boy's face. It was as white as a sheet of paper. But he wasn't making a sound, just biting fiercely into his lip. He was, though Jamie didn't recognize it, in a state of shock.

By now, other players were rushing across to see for themselves what had happened. Yet, oddly enough, none of the Dinthorpe side made any attempt to manhandle Jamie or even remonstrate with him. Most of them, too, were silenced, even awed, by the sight of their stricken team-mate. Several of them sensed that it was not only the end of the match for him: it could well be the end of his entire football season, at the very least. The fact that he wasn't making any sound at all was the most frightening aspect of his injury.

'Billy, Billy, Billy,' his skipper was saying to him, over and over again, as he knelt beside him. 'Tell us how you're feeling, mate.'

After one quick glance, the referee turned aside for a private word with Billy's manager, whose acceleration on the pitch had taken him past Jonathan Fixby.

'It's a bad one, I'm afraid, a fracture almost certainly,' the official told him. 'Can you cope till an ambulance gets here?'

The manager nodded and tapped the bag he was carrying. 'I've done a first aid course and I always have an inflatable splint handy in here. I hope, Ref, you're going to deal properly with the young hooligan who caused this. I know what I'd do with him.'

'Don't worry,' was all the ref replied.

By now Jamie was sitting on the pitch, having his own injury, the doubly bruised ankle, attended to by Mr Fixby. As soon as he reached Jamie the coach had drawn him aside and then brusquely told him to sit down. He wasn't to conceal his pain but, above all, he was to be apologetic and mild and remorseful when, as was bound to happen, the referee came over to deal with him. This wasn't the moment for the coach to tell the player what he himself thought of the offence. That would come later, whatever punishment the referee awarded.

The pain-killing spray had been applied and the agony was receding. Jamie sat and listened and tried to rid his mind of the expression on Billy's face. His own anger at what Billy had done to him had completely vanished. They'd both been at fault, he was well aware of that, but he had survived the clash; Billy hadn't.

'What's your name, Number 12?'

Even though he had his notebook out, in which he already had Jamie's name as Denholm's substitute, the referee couldn't refrain from asking that question. Jamie told him and waited for the onslaught.

'There's only one word to describe what you did, Austerby: criminal. No other word will do. Don't you agree?'

Jamie hesitated. He shot a quick glance at Jonathan Fixby, now leaning back on his heels, but he got no help there.

'Er, I'm sorry, Ref. Truly sorry.'

As instructed, he was being contrite.

'Sorry's not enough, Austerby, not for what you've done to that lad over there. It's a long time since I saw a worse case of violent conduct. And that's what you're guilty of.'

'But he started it, Ref. I mean, he whacked me twice, deliberately. I – I can hardly walk.'

Jamie could tell just how feeble his excuse sounded but he felt he had to say something in mitigation. Jonathan Fixby was all too plainly avoiding his eye. There was going to be no help, no sympathy even, from that quarter.

'I hoped you were going to be decent enough not to try to justify your deplorable conduct,' the referee told him with bitterness. 'I can see you haven't got that in you. Anyway, I'm not wasting any more of my time on you. I'm sending you off the field of play for violent conduct, and a full report will be sent to the secretary of the Sunday League. The disciplinary committee will doubtless see that justice is done in your case.'

He paused and then, looking at the Denholm coach, added witheringly: 'If he claims he can't walk, Mr Fixby, then I must ask you to remove him yourself, forthwith.'

Without another glance at Jamie he stalked away to see what was being done for Billy, now almost completely surrounded by players from both teams. Someone had been despatched to the farmhouse to phone for the ambulance while others were looking for a makeshift stretcher.

'Can you walk, do you think?' Jonathan Fixby asked Jamie. 'You're not going to get any sympathy even if you can't, so you might as well try.'

With a helping hand from the coach, Jamie got to his feet, wincing more with the anticipation than the reality of pain. He knew his ankle would swell up again and he wished he could put it in a bucket of ice. If only Vicky had been there she'd have seen what was needed and answered that need. In the present climate Jamie knew he couldn't ask for special treatment from Mr Fixby. Already the ankle was discolouring again.

'Keep clear of their casualty,' Fixby told him as they moved awkwardly towards the touchline. 'You can't improve matters by trying to tell him you're sorry, even if he's in a fit state to hear you. You're only likely to inflame feelings in the rest of their team.'

It occurred to Jamie, then, that none of his own teammates had come up to show any sympathy for *him*. Those who weren't crowded around Billy were standing to one side, discussing the probable fate of the two involved in the clash. They knew that Jamie had been sent off, and that, naturally, the coach didn't look pleased with life, to say the least, and so they thought it was best to say and do nothing that might later be misinterpreted. Having seen the extent of the injury to Billy, they could hardly condone what Jamie had done. The cynics among them could argue that because he'd got himself sent off he'd let his own side down: for the rest of the match Denholm Avengers would be down to ten men.

As Jamie limped to the changing-rooms Dinthorpe's substitute, the boy who'd gone to telephone, returned with a tarpaulin which he and a squad of team-mates spread out on the pitch and then carefully re-folded to make a conveyance for Billy.

When, after the long delay, the game at last was resumed it was interrupted again within two minutes by the arrival of the ambulance. There was some discussion as to who should accompany Billy to the hospital and at one point it was even suggested that Jamie should go. Dinthorpe's manager couldn't because he drove the team's minibus and the substitute was needed to take Billy's place on the field. In the end, Billy had only the ambulancemen for company but the promise was made that he would be visited as soon as the game was over.

The fire had gone out of it when the game really got going again. Neither side seemed able to produce skill or commitment and when an infringement occurred it was always accidental and apologies abounded. Dinthorpe's luck was still out, for when they did break through the opposition's defence weak shooting, poor timing, ill-placed divots or just good goalkeeping kept the ball out of Denholm's net. The forwards in red-and-black quickly sensed that it wasn't going to be their day, either.

Denholm's ten players really didn't have to exert themselves much to restrict Dinthorpe's scoring opportunities. Initially, Ian Pickering dropped back into midfield to help break up the expected assault forces; but his presence wasn't needed and Jonathan Fixby waved him back into his usual striker's role. So he quite enjoyed himself running at Dinthorpe's increasingly apathetic defence and then varying his tactics by testing the goalie with long-range shots. He had the feeling that if he really persevered he'd notch his second goal of the match. Ninety seconds before the final whistle sounded, he did. From a long clearance the ball bounced invitingly on the edge of the penalty area, where Ian collected it, sidestepped a couple of half-hearted challenges and then drove it high into the net.

Banned from the touchline by virtue of being sent off, Jamie watched the final stages of the match from the window of the changing-room. He felt just as forlorn as he looked. He would have enjoyed a shower, all the more so because he was on his own and could have lingered in the heat. Sometimes after a match, and especially after a good win, the wildness in the showers got out of hand. It was just his luck this time that there was no hot water. So, after a quick and unsatisfactory clean-up, he changed and then watched his team-mates complete their remarkable triumph.

They trooped into the changing-room in good spirits, the sickening injury to the Dinthorpe full-back now a thing of the past. They had not only defeated tough and renowned opponents but collected valuable points to lift them up the League table. They had every reason to feel like enjoying themselves. Jamie came in for a few jibes but most of the players seemed unsure how to treat him. Guy Kelton, who'd stayed out on the touchline with Jonathan Fixby, was the only one to offer what sounded to Jamie like genuine sympathy.

'Don't blame you at all for what you did,' he said quietly. 'Both full-backs were murder to play against, weren't they? You must have been unlucky to, er, injure him like you did. You could just as easily have caught him on the boot or the shinguard and then he wouldn't have been hurt at all. Look at what I got, anyway.'

He rolled down his sock and the evidence of the bruising tackles he received in the match was unmistakable. Jamie nodded his understanding but didn't reciprocate by displaying his own wounds. He knew Ian Pickering was watching them and he'd be sure to scoff. Although he wasn't of a powerful build – quite the reverse really, for someone had recently described him as 'that skinny striker' – Ian generally appeared indestructible.

Jamie wandered over to the bench where Steve Derome was pulling off his shirt and sat down.

'You ever broken a leg, Steve?' he asked quietly.

The midfielder shook his head.

'Well, do you know anybody who has? You know, how bad the pain was and all that? How long it takes to get over it – if – if it isn't a really bad break?'

Steve appeared to consider the matter.

'There was a lad at my first school broke his arm. Playground accident. I saw it happen. But he soon seemed to get over it. Just complained that he had a lot of, well, itching under the plaster. 'Course, we all signed it, the plaster,

45

I mean. When they took it off Simon was right as any-thing. Couldn't tell he'd broken it. Look, Jamie, don't let that accident out there today get you down. These things could happen to anybody, any one of us. No good heaping all the blame on yourself. That guy got what he deserved, really.'

Jamie couldn't agree with that view and he was about to say so when he caught sight of Mr Fixby frowning at him from the other side of the room where he'd been having a look at John Blakiston's scalp.

'No damage, son,' the coach reported. 'Tough as an old tree, your nut!'

'Yeah, and just as thick!' cracked Stuart Elcro.

John waved a fist at the goalkeeper in mock anger. Those two went in for long-running jokes about each other.

Jonathan Fixby took Jamie on one side and began to speak so quietly that even Jamie himself had difficulty in hearing him at first. But the urgency of the coach's tone didn't allow for an invitation to speak up.

'Look, son, I told you I can't condone what you did. That still goes. But I've got to think of your own good, and the good of the team. If you dwell on the injury to their full-back you'll finish up getting depressed. That's no good to you and it's no good to me. What's happened can't be undone. You've just got to accept that accidents do happen. So – '

'But it *wasn't* really an accident, Boss!' Jamie cut in. 'I mean, I didn't *intend* to break his leg but I did lash out because he'd hurt me.'

The coach nodded and resumed his statement. 'I know

that, and you'll be punished for your crime. No doubt about that. But I'm talking about the *effect* of the thing that happened. I don't want you to brood about it and I don't want you to try and make amends by going to see Billy in hospital or at his home or wherever he is. No good can come of that. His parents might even duff you up if they see you! Believe me, they might. Feeling sympathy is all very well, son, but it has to come to an end at some point, so you might as well start thinking of the future for yourself now. Life doesn't come to a full stop for *anybody* just because of one broken leg. Broken legs happen every day, probably dozens of 'em. People get over them. And you've got to get over this and start looking ahead again.'

He paused and looked Jamie straight in the eyes. 'OK, son? Got the message?'

'I think so,' Jamie answered, with no note of confidence in his voice.

The coach touched him on the shoulder.

'Good. Then I'll expect to see you down for training next week as usual.'

Jamie, left on his own, decided it was time to go home. He picked up his kit and set off for the bus stop.

Steve caught up with him just before he reached the gate out of the sports field and fell into step.

'Did the Great Fixer tell you anything sensational?' he wanted to know.

Jamie shook his head.

'No, just what you'd expect. Try and forget the whole thing. But that's impossible because I'll be thinking about it every time I look at a League table or see a bloke with his leg in plaster. I'll also get at least a one-match ban for being sent off, so that'll remind me about it again, won't it, when I'm watching instead of playing for the Avengers?'

'Yeah, it's tough, really tough,' Steve murmured. He hesitated a moment or two and then went on: 'Look, I hate to ask you this *now*, Jamie, but could you possibly lend me some money? Say a fiver? Honest, I'll pay you back in a week, no danger.'

'A fiver! Where do you think I'm going to get that sort of money from? And what do you want it for?'

'Oh come on, Jamie, you know you're never short of cash.' Steve sounded irritated at having to spell things out. 'You've said yourself that your dad's generous when his business is doing well – and you told us the other day that things are so good he's just added another truck to his fleet. So – '

'It's not exactly a fleet, Steve. It's only his third lorry. And it has to be paid for before it earns much for the haulage business. So Dad hasn't got that much to spare. Anyway, I need all the loot I can get. Saving up.'

'Saving up? What for?'

'Instruments, and all the gear. We're planning to form a group, you know. Some mates of mine at the Youth Club. Everything we'll need'll cost a fortune.'

'Where'll you perform, if you get this group going?'

Jamie shrugged. 'Don't know. We haven't even got a *name* for it yet. But we'll get organized soon. Tim's absolutely great on the guitar.'

Steve didn't want to know about that. He had only one thing on his mind.

'Right, well, I'll have to find another mate to tap. So, see you around, Jamie.'

'I expect so. Unless I get banned for the rest of the season.'

Four

When, just over a fortnight later, Jamie returned home from a wasted evening at the Youth Club, Vicky was lying curled up on the sofa in the sitting-room, but he ignored her as he crossed to the television set and switched it on. A news programme, in which a familiar politician was being interviewed about still more familiar financial crises, came up first; and so Jamie chased through the channels to find something better. And failed.

He stumped across the room again, switched off noisily, fiddled with the stereo, put on something loud and then dropped heavily into a protesting chair, not for effect but because that was how he felt.

'Do you know,' Vicky began, raising her voice only to a level where it would be heard, 'some people actually like a little quiet when they're reading. That's why they choose a quiet room in the first place. Even, I might add, when they're reading rubbish.'

'In the first place,' he retaliated, deliberately echoing her words, 'you shouldn't be reading rubbish. Not some-one who's supposed to be intelligent.'

'If you don't read rubbish sometimes,' she answered

with a grin, 'you don't know how to appreciate the good stuff.'

'I didn't know there *was* any good stuff around here,' he said glumly.

Vicky uncurled her bare legs, sat up sharply and, very accurately, pitched the magazine she'd been reading into the copper-coloured waste-paper bin beside the fireplace.

'The trouble with you, old brother, is that you can't see good in *anything* these days,' she told him, frowning intensely. 'You just moon around finding misery everywhere. You're like a – like a wet blanket on a clothes-line, sagging in the middle and dripping over everything.'

'You'd sag in the middle if you'd been banned from playing in the Sunday League for *four* matches! You'd hit the roof.'

'Look, it's not the end of the world, Jamie. You've already missed one match, so you're a quarter of the way through your – your sentence. In another month you'll have forgotten all about it.'

'Forget, forget, forget!' he almost shouted. 'That's all anybody ever says about anything I've done. But I don't forget, nobody forgets. Everybody goes on and on reminding me what happened. *Bonebreaker*, that's what some of my own team-mates call me now. *Bonebreaker*, so how can you get anything out of your mind when they call you that?'

Vicky thought for a moment or two and then said: 'Well, *some* guys wouldn't mind getting a nickname like that. I mean, it makes you sound really *powerful*. So what's wrong with that?'

That, to Jamie's mind, was a stupid point of view and he

51

wasn't even going to respond to it. He got up and returned to the stereo to change the sound. But it wasn't a night when anything could please him.

'How did you and Tim get on with your plans for the group?' asked Vicky, kindly changing the subject. 'Have you fixed up a place for a rehearsal yet?'

'No point.'

She sighed deeply. His attitude was beginning to annoy her, but she wanted to help him out of his mood. 'Why not?'

'Karl's father won't come up with the money he promised for the drums. He says Karl has to get some money of his own together before he makes his contribution. But he *knows* we need it now and we'll pay it back later. We only want a loan, not a load of hand-outs.'

'So what are you going to do about it?'

'Haven't a clue. Tim thinks we should go and find somebody who'll hire us the oldest, rottenest, cheapest set of drums in existence, just so we can make a start. I don't agree. You've got to do things properly. We'll never be a success if we start with rubbish like that. If we take a pride in what we're doing, what we're playing, our own instruments, then we'll be good. I know. Tim's just impatient. We had a ding-dong argument.'

'Did you fall out with him, then?'

'Yeah, I suppose you could say that.'

'I'm not surprised,' said Vicky. But she said it so softly that he wouldn't be able to hear it against the background music.

The next day, Jamie fell out with someone else.

The ban imposed by the disciplinary committee of the Sunday League didn't, of course, extend to school matches. Accordingly, Jamie was, as usual, chosen for his school's second team for what Ross Peterson, the sports master, described as 'a truly vital game'. In fact, it was a county Cup-tie, a second round match, and Mr Peterson was eager to collect the trophy that lay at the end of that particular sporting road.

The game was being played, immediately after school was ended for the day, on Redfield's own pitch, and their opponents, Quarrington, had travelled from the other end of the county. With his usual thoroughness in preparing for events, Mr Peterson had checked up on Quarrington's capabilities. Thus, before his team went out on to the pitch he expressed the firm view that Redfield should have no difficulty in winning, like 'a thoroughbred horse racing against donkeys: in no danger of defeat at any stage of the race'.

At which point Kieran Mallaby turned to Jamie and murmured: 'Unless the horse falls down and breaks a leg. Result: donkey wins in a canter.'

If Kieran had heard about Jamie's disastrous experience in the Dinthorpe match he'd forgotten all about it. He cracked jokes all the time, especially when they could be aimed at the sports master, of whom Kieran didn't have a high opinion at any time. But then Kieran never lacked confidence in his own considerable abilities (both on and off the sports field) and so he felt he was in a position to pass judgment on, as he saw them, lesser mortals. Usually he was complimentary about Jamie's play.

Jamie knew that Kieran had made the remark innocently but he couldn't get it out of his mind as the teams met to shake hands, exchange pennants and then engage in combat. This was his first serious match since playing for the Avengers against Dinthorpe and he wanted to enjoy it. Everyone at home and at school who knew about the notorious incident had carefully avoided mentioning it in the past few days, as if collectively aware that too much had been made of it already. Jamie had been fearful of catching sight of the victim himself, Billy Howard, in the town or on a bus or even coming up the path to the Austerbys' front door to demand retribution. Billy Howard was always somewhere on the perimeter of his mind.

His own injuries had cleared quite quickly, even without the aid this time of Vicky's ministrations. He couldn't help thinking that was a bit unfair when he remembered how Billy must be suffering. The fear that surfaced from time to time was that he himself would break a leg at soccer. Then, no doubt, people would say that justice had been done.

Mr Peterson had ordered his team to attack from the outset. Quarrington, he pointed out in a typically school-masterly phrase, 'had to be taught a lesson.' He didn't think it necessary to explain what lesson he had in mind. It was spitting rain when the game kicked-off and that added to the treacherousness of a surface already made slippery by heavy rain earlier in the week. The cold snap had ended the day after Denholm's victory over Dinthorpe.

In the opening minutes both sides found it virtually im-possible to string two passes together and the Redfield supporters lining both touchlines had little to cheer. The

Headmaster had made it plain in that morning's assembly that he expected support for the team even though the match was being played outside normal school hours. Cynics had already pointed out, though, that the Head himself wasn't present. Almost five minutes went by before Jamie got a touch of the ball. And that's all it was: a touch. The ball was deflected in his direction from a sliced clearance out of Quarrington's penalty area. It was spinning when he tried to bring it under control and all that happened was that it skidded into touch from his toe-cap for a throw-in for the other side.

'Get a grip, Austerby!' Mr Peterson yelled, to demonstrate, more than anything else, that he was in command.

Some of the younger spectators, no doubt keen to be in Mr Peterson's good books, laughed or, in one or two cases, jeered and repeated the message. Jamie felt like responding with a rude gesture to show his contempt for such conduct but wisely decided against it. At that moment the Head was seen to be making his way towards the pitch.

The ball was punted fairly aimlessly up and down the field for prolonged spells and it appeared that nobody, to use Peterson's phrase, was getting a grip on the match. His belief that the match should be little more than an exercise canter for Redfield was, on present evidence, thoroughly misplaced. Quarrington, encouraged by the absence of any real challenge from the home side, began to increase the tempo of their own play. A determined, weaving run by their right-winger was rounded off neatly when his accurate cross was headed firmly against the crossbar by Quarrington's athletic striker. Had he aimed only a few centimetres lower the ball would surely have finished in the back of the net, for the goalkeeper was badly positioned to make a save. Ross Peterson had two complaints about that incident: one, understandably, was against the goalkeeper; the second was against Jamie Austerby for not tackling the winger more decisively in the first place. Jamie had moved in on his opposite number and tried to dispossess him. He'd almost succeeded but, a trifle luckily, the Quarrington player had regained control of the ball before Jamie could make use of it.

Jamie himself didn't give a second thought to the matter: he wasn't a defender and couldn't be expected to tackle effectively, especially when he was up against a good ball-player. He'd tried to get the ball and it was enough that he'd come so close to his success.

By the end of the first quarter of this dull, even ponderous, match he was not only feeling starved of a decent pass but chilled. The rain had intensified and conditions were becoming more unpleasant by the minute. He began slapping his arms against his sides to get warm. If someone saw that as an invitation to send a pass that would be fine by him. But then, when the ball did reach him from one of his team-mates, he failed to make much progress. He managed to outwit the first opponent who came at him, but the second swept in like a runaway steer and the two of them fell in a heap with the ball running loose. It was an obvious foul and one was promptly awarded. Neither Jamie nor his adversary had suffered at all in the collision and the Quarrington player amiably offered to shake hands as a sort of apology. Jamie was turning away at that point, wiping mud off his knee, and didn't see the gesture.

56

At half-time Ross Peterson was on the verge of exploding.

'You're dreadful, all of you, absolutely dreadful,' he said hotly as soon as he had the team grouped round him in the middle of the pitch. 'I don't know what you've been thinking of but it hasn't been football, or how to win a game. No ideas, no push, no urgency, no nothing. Even no sportsmanship in your case, Austerby!'

'Pardon?' Jamie was completely taken aback by that comment.

'You heard me! When an opponent holds out his hand to shake after a bit of a dust-up then the real sportsman *shakes it*. Doesn't ignore it and try to make the other chap look foolish. I'm not having that sort of attitude in my team, Austerby, so you can cut it out right away. In this school, success and sportsmanship should walk hand in hand.'

Someone giggled at that until Mr Peterson tried to pin the culprit down with a gimlet glance. It wasn't Jamie. He still didn't know what the sports master was talking about but sensed that it was prudent not to ask any questions.

'We've got to *work* at this game and really pile on the pressure,' Peterson concluded after firing off a few more cutting comments. 'You've got to go and *seek* the ball, not just wait for it to roll invitingly, obligingly, in your direction. And that applies to you in particular, young Austerby. Don't just – '

'But I'm supposed to be on the wing. I'm supposed to go down the touchline, down to the by-line. That's what you told me before the match began.'

'Every player has to adapt to changing circumstances,'

the sports master replied blandly (and untruthfully in the light of the orders he often gave about *sticking* to instructions). 'If the ball isn't reaching you then you must go and get it. Otherwise you're a complete passenger, and therefore useless. Which is what you've been so far this afternoon.'

Before Jamie could make another protest, Peterson switched his attention to Kieran Mallaby who, he said, was doing well, but not quite well enough. He wanted Redfield's chief striker to be a little more positive, a little greedier on the ball. Kieran, who must have felt like making a joke in response, for once just nodded.

'Honestly, that man's a total hypocrite!' Jamie exploded in Kieran's ear when they were out of earshot of the sports master. 'If things don't work out just as he wants them – and immediately – he starts blaming everyone but himself. He should have told me he wanted me to have a roaming role.'

'Well, if you're going to roam, don't take the ball out of sight,' Kieran replied. 'I need the ball to score with.'

The rain hadn't relented by the time the second half began. Water was beginning to lie on the surface, causing players to skid unpredictably whether or not they had the ball.

'You didn't tell me we were playing at water polo!' the Head remarked loudly to Ross Peterson.

Everyone around them laughed almost hysterically at such wit from such a source.

For Redfield supporters, it was the last amusing thing to happen for some time. Quarrington, apparently inspired by the half-time talk from their leader, booted the ball as hard as they could upfield and, in force, charged after it. The tactics were crude but fruitful. Redfield, taken aback by such numbers, couldn't contrive to keep possession or clear their lines. Suddenly, it seemed to the defenders, attackers were swarming all over them. Ross Peterson was signalling vainly for his own forwards to drop back to give support when Quarrington's right-back swung the ball into the penalty area yet again. The goalie came off his line to punch, missed the ball, lost his footing and was lying helpless as an opponent thumped the ball into the empty net.

Quarrington's joy didn't last too long. They were composed enough to cope with Redfield's immediate, and anticipated, retaliation. The big boot was employed now to aid defence. Jamie, diligently pursuing the ball as he'd been told to, exchanged a crisp one-two with Kieran in a raid through the middle but then failed to get much power behind his shot at goal. The Quarrington 'keeper turned the ball away with ease. Half a minute later Jamie had the ball once more on the edge of the box where he was in a position to shoot again; but before he could swing his foot a defender barged into him. No foul was awarded this time, though Jamie had lost possession.

Moments later Jamie was astonished to see that the referee was beckoning to him. Surely he couldn't possibly have committed an offence! Yet again, he himself had been the victim of a bad tackle. But then the referee changed his signal and pointed to the touchline. Where, arms aloft and plainly calling him in, Ross Peterson stood. For a second or two it didn't dawn on Jamie what was happening. Then, like a sledgehammer, it hit him . . .

He was being substituted!

Andy Vardy, a fresh-faced younger boy, charged across to take his place in attack. He and Jamie brushed hands as they passed but Jamie was so stunned he forgot to wish Andy luck. Ross Peterson didn't deign to notice him as Jamie crossed the touchline, turned and watched his teammates struggle to get on level terms with Quarrington.

Soon the word was passed along the touchline to set up a chant in an effort to lift the team and 'Red-FIELD, Red-FIELD' rang out rhythmically. Even the Head appeared to be joining in. Jamie, though, found he hadn't the voice at present. Choked was how he felt. Somehow, the humiliation of being substituted was just as great as when he was sent off against Dinthorpe. He couldn't deny that he deserved to be dismissed for breaking Billy Howard's leg; but his form in the match with Quarrington was definitely no worse than that of most of the Redfield players. So why had he been removed from the field? The answer, in his view, was obvious: Mr Peterson needed to find a scapegoat for Redfield's poor performance, and he'd been selected because he'd stood up to the sports master on the matter of tactical play. He was being punished for daring to voice an opinion different from Peterson's.

Then, just as the referee was looking at his watch and calculating how long to the final whistle, Redfield scored the desperately desired equalizer. It was achieved by the individual brilliance of Kieran Mallaby; but the crucial pass was supplied by Andy Vardy, Jamie's replacement. Andy, sensing a chance to get involved in the game, darted in from the wing to challenge for a fifty-fifty ball – and emerged from a fierce body contact as the victor.

Spotting Kieran accelerating, he slid the ball through the mud: it was placed behind the nearest defender and directly into the striker's path.

In spite of the clinging conditions, Kieran kept close control and, when threatened, jinked first one way, then the other. Quarrington's defence couldn't retreat fast enough to cope with this attack. As Kieran burst into the penalty area the goalie, now short of cover, decided he must come out and try to smother the ball at the attacker's feet. Kieran couldn't have asked for anything better. He maintained his course to meet the advancing goalie head-on and then, feinting to go one way, he turned to his left and calmly hooked the ball over the diving goalie's head and into the back of the net. It was a long time since anyone present had seen a cooler, or more clinical, bit of goal-scoring.

'Just what we deserved, just what we deserved!' Ross Peterson exulted.

That was hardly true, but no one supporting Redfield was going to dispute it. They were still in the Cup and that was all that mattered. When the team came off the pitch Jamie was uncertain about joining in the celebrations. But, for appearances' sake, he had to do something so that Ross Peterson wouldn't be able to accuse him of sulking or of showing poor sportsmanship. Yet, because he wasn't on the playing area when the goal was scored, he felt quite numb about the whole thing.

'Terrific goal, Kier, must be one of your greatest,' he congratulated the school's latest instant hero.

Kieran, surrounded by admirers, barely acknowledged the compliment. He was half-listening to Ross Peterson, who had one arm round Andy Vardy's shoulders and was babbling about 'twin strikers of the future'. The sports master was already making his plans for the replay at Quarrington the following week.

Jamie was turning away when an arm descended on his shoulder.

'Well, what happened to *you* in the game? When I couldn't spot you on the pitch I thought you must have missed the game.'

'Dad! Hey, I didn't know you were coming this way today.'

'Finished a trip a bit earlier than I thought I would. So I dropped in to see how you were getting on because I remembered you were playing this Cup-tie.'

'Are you in the new truck then?' Jamie cut in quickly before his father could repeat his original question. When he received a nod in reply he added: 'Oh, great, then you can give me a lift home! I really fancy a go in this one, you know, so I want to see how everything works – and where everything is. I mean, that dashboard looks as if it's been borrowed from Concorde!'

His father laughed. 'All in good time, Jamie, all in good time. You know the courts'd ban me for life if I allowed someone of your age to get loose in one of my trucks.'

'But that abandoned airfield I was mentioning, Dad. Nobody would see us there early one morning if – '

'Jamie! The rest of the players have gone in! If you're going to have a shower or something you'd better get going before all the hot water's gone. I'm parked down Hoo Lane. Don't be too long. I could eat two teas already.'

By the time he reached the dressing-room Jamie was feeling distinctly cheerful. And, surprisingly, hungry. That, he decided, was because his father had mentioned food. Unlike many long-distance drivers, David Austerby didn't eat much when he was actually driving. He was devoted to his wife's cooking (so much so that it was something of a running joke with business contacts as well as with friends and within the family). So, whenever he could get home for a meal, he did.

Now that he had three trucks, and therefore hired other drivers, Mr Austerby had to spend an increasing amount of time in the office in order to run his business; but, whenever possible, he liked to do a trip himself, especially in the highly sophisticated new vehicle. Although his business activities prevented him from attending as many of his children's sporting fixtures as he would have liked, he turned up to cheer them on when the opportunity arose. He was well aware that for all her obvious enthusiasms and sudden passions for new skills and techniques, Vicky treated sport a good deal more casually than Jamie did. Vicky soon got over setbacks and disappointments, however desperate they seemed at the time. Not so Jamie. It was one of Jamie's weaknesses (yet, also, one of his strengths) that he tended to take too much of life too seriously. He would brood over things that he should have dismissed swiftly from his mind. So, as often as it could be managed, David Austerby 'talked things through', as he put it, with his son. Problems could be resolved in that way; and even when they couldn't at least a balance of understanding of the nature of a problem could be reached.

Jamie decided against having a shower. He was, he told himself, damp enough already. His one thought was to get changed, get to the truck and then get home. Some of his team-mates were still fooling around in the spray when Jamie, zipping up his sports bag while on the move, was stepping out into the corridor.

'Austerby!' Mr Peterson called. 'Were we all so bad that you can no longer bear to have anything to do with us?'

'Sorry, sir, but I thought we were all finished,' replied Jamie politely, ignoring the heavy sarcasm. 'My dad's waiting to pick me up.'

'Well, we're not all finished, as you put it. I'm about to discuss plans for the replay.' He paused calculatedly, and then went on: 'Still, as those plans don't involve you, you *are* finished. So you can go on your way, rejoicing or otherwise.'

Jamie turned and walked briskly away. It was a jolt to be told he wasn't even being considered for the team's next match, but it was what he might have expected. Once you were out of favour with Peterson it took a long time for him to recognize you as a human being again. Reviewing the match, Jamie knew he could have tried to hold on to the ball a little longer on the few times it came his way. He could have tried to win it in tackles more often. But, on such a surface, his speed, one of his prime assets, would have been blunted. He couldn't have given the rest of the forwards the sort of service they usually expected from him.

One thing he didn't admit to himself: that, whenever he was involved in bodily contact with an opponent, he had checked himself instead of going through with his effort.

64

In everything he attempted, he hadn't tried as hard as he usually tried.

Was he losing his nerve? Had he become a – a coward? The word came into his mind and it surprised him so much he actually gulped. For a moment or two he paused on the path that led across waste land to Hoo Lane. Would anyone really think, and *say*, that he was chickening out of physical challenges on the pitch? It hardly seemed possible. Yet, with people like Ross Peterson and Jonathan Fixby, to whom results seemed to mean everything, you never really knew what they were thinking.

Jamie's thoughts drifted back to the day he'd rescued Vicky's adored stray cat from the top of a tree in a copse near their home. Unpredictably, crazily, the black cat had shot up there in pursuit of a particular bird it was determined to catch. Then, of course, it had realized its predicament and was too terrified to attempt to descend. Vicky, then only about eight, was almost demented with grief because she was convinced the creature would not be able to hold on and would fall to its death. So, instead of sensibly calling for professional help, Jamie had climbed to get it even though he was never very keen on heights. Always he had to steel himself not to look down. The cat seemed to go berserk when at last he got within reach of it, and he had to cope with its claws and its teeth as well as difficult handholds and footholds. He couldn't count the times he was sure he, and then they, would go crashing to the ground and be killed outright. At the topmost point they must have been thirty feet above the ground. But, in the end, bitten and scratched by the cat, and stabbed and scratched by branches, he'd restored the creature to

Vicky's grateful arms. Two weeks later it was killed right outside their house by a passing car. A man taking a walk through the copse had stopped to watch the rescue and when it was over came up to Jamie to say: 'That took real guts on your part, sonny. I could see you and the cat were scared to death of each other as well as scared of falling.'

His other brave feat, as he remembered it, was achieved about the same time, though in the winter rather than in the spring of that year. For a dare he'd walked across a frozen pond. Only the previous month the ice had cracked under the weight of another boy and he'd very nearly drowned (or so the victim claimed publicly and often). Jamie had carefully planned his attempt and wore a buoyancy belt under a thick sweater. He didn't know whether that would actually save him if plunged into the pond but it was better than taking no precautions at all. As it turned out, he didn't get even one foot wet. True enough, the ice cracked, and the noise alone was good for his reputation afterwards as by-standers reminisced about his success. But it held long enough for him to complete his walk and scale the shallow earth bank on the other side of the pond. He often remembered how long and how thuddingly his heart bumped once he was back on firm ground. Nobody else dared follow his example. So he had hero status for a long time.

Now, as he turned into Hoo Lane, he felt dispirited by such recollections. Would anyone ever regard him as courageous again? Or would people think he had no guts at all on a soccer pitch? Even more to the point at the moment: when would he play in another football game? Banned from the Sunday League and dropped from the school's second team, he appeared to have no immediate future as a player at all.

The sight of his father's shiningly new truck cheered him a little. The silver and blue livery had always appealed to him and he thoroughly approved of the legend painted on the side of each vehicle: 'Be transported the Austerby way.'

The engine, which hardly made any more noise than a refrigerator, was already running before Jamie climbed into the spacious cab – spacious enough to contain sleeping accommodation when needed – and so as soon as the door closed they were off.

From such an elevated position Jamie was able to look down on his school friends and give a regal wave if any of them spotted him. With rain still falling, however, few boys were taking much notice of passing trucks and those riding in them. A glimpse of one boy suddenly reminded David Austerby of something he wanted to mention to Jamie.

'I notice your pal Steve Derome wasn't playing today,' he said casually.

'No, that's right. We missed him. I missed him particularly. Steve makes sure I get the ball now and again! Not like the dope who was in his place today.'

'Is Steve injured, then?'

'No, he had a dental appointment. Been having trouble with one of his back teeth. I must say, he could've picked a better time to be away.'

'Was he having a lot of pain?'

'Yeah, he said so.'

'Well, he seemed to have recovered when I saw him as I

was driving through town. He was having a very intense conversation with a girl, arguing with her, even *pleading* perhaps. Intense, anyway. I was stopped at the traffic lights in Bank Street, so I had plenty of opportunity of observing them.'

'Steve, with a girl? When was this, Dad? I mean, what time?' Jamie was genuinely puzzled.

'Oh, about twenty minutes before the match ended, I suppose. I must say, she was a very noticeable girl. Masses of coppery-coloured hair. Didn't you know he had a girl-friend?'

'Definitely not. He hasn't said anything to me about any girl.'

'Well, the whole scene looked, er, interesting. Perhaps his dental appointment was cancelled after all and he'd just met an old friend by chance.'

Jamie didn't know what to make of this piece of news. He hadn't seen much of Steve lately, not even at school, and so he wasn't sure what he was up to these days. In the past they'd been close enough to confide in each other their fears and aspirations in various aspects of life besides sport. They'd gone on trips to famous football and cricket grounds and hunted for autographs together. Recently, it seemed to Jamie on reflection, Steve had been detaching himself from his usual group of cronies. He wasn't even showing his usual interest in Denholm Avengers. And then, of course, he'd twice in a little more than a fortnight asked Jamie to lend him money. In itself, that wasn't completely out of character, because Steve often claimed he was short of cash. The latest requests, however, had contained a hint of desperation, as though Steve was in trouble. Afterwards, Jamie had felt guilty at not helping his friend out, despite the fact that he himself was in need of every pound he could lay his hands on for the instruments his pop-group-to-be needed. But he should have made more effort to help a friend. He made a resolution to let Steve have some cash if he asked for a loan again.

'You were really lost in your own deep thoughts then, did you know that?' Mr Austerby remarked.

'Sorry, Dad.'

Jamie looked up to see his father regarding him quizzically. Then, in a familiar gesture, David Austerby pushed back the American baseball cap he favoured from time to time and scratched his head. Jamie realized that a leading question was about to be put to him.

'Sure you haven't got a girl-friend you don't talk to us about?'

The question was so surprising that for a moment or two Jamie simply couldn't think how to answer. He stalled.

'What?'

'I said, have you got a girl-friend, one you haven't mentioned to anybody? Look, Jamie, this isn't an interrogation or anything like that. I'm not *prying*. I'm just interested. After all, it's not unnatural these days for a boy of your age to be interested in girls. *Everything* seems to start younger these days. You and Steve wouldn't be exceptions from what I've seen.'

'Oh, definitely not,' Jamie replied emphatically. 'Having a sister like Vicky is quite enough for me to cope with, thanks!'

His father laughed.

'Yes, I know what you mean. She's a live wire all right.

Goodness knows what life will be like when she's old enough to take up with boys.'

For the rest of the journey they talked about family matters, much to Jamie's relief. It helped him to forget the miseries of the afternoon on the football pitch. When they reached home it was immediately obvious that Vicky had some vital news to impart to her brother.

'You'll never guess,' she declared with such eagerness that she allowed him no time to try. 'But I've fixed up a terrific game for you. You're playing in a hockey match on Saturday week – a *mixed* team, boys and girls together. So how about that to keep you on your sporting toes now you can't play footie?'

Five

'Jamie, I'd like a word, if you don't mind, before you push off home,' Jonathan Fixby said quietly as the Denholm players trooped off the pitch after an evening training session. 'I expect you've got homework to do but I won't keep you long. OK?'

'Right, Boss,' Jamie replied almost automatically.

It was not unusual for the coach to have a quiet word with one of his players, whether it was after a match or training, but Jamie sensed that this wasn't going to be an ordinary 'chat' about future team strategy or the need to remedy some weakness in his play on or off the ball. He hadn't, he realized, been at his best during the training spell; from the outset, he'd felt in low spirits. There was a reason for that but he didn't want to recognize it. But, certainly, nothing had gone right for him whatever he tried: his timing, his passing, even his judgment about when to part with the ball or attempt a challenge, all seemed to be wrong. Team-mates, quite understandably, had displayed irritation at what he was failing to do. Twice, at least, he'd been shouted at with real anger. He'd apologized but hadn't been able to improve with his next centre or flicked pass through the middle.

Jonathan Fixby was going to tear a strip off him, either for lack of effort or loss of concentration, or both. That was inevitable, in Jamie's view. Well, he'd just take it, he would just listen and let the Boss say what he had to say. There wouldn't be much point in arguing. Jonathan wouldn't really want to hear someone else's point of view.

'Well, how do you think things went tonight?' was Fixby's first question when he and Jamie were the only two left in the changing-rooms. It was put so softly that Jamie was immediately suspicious. This was surely the prelude to fierce condemnation of his own performance.

'Not so good really, I don't think anyone was on top form,' was the careful reply. 'Perhaps it was a reaction after Sunday's defeat at Odlington. I mean, I know I was not playing in that match but I felt the rest of the lads were still thinking about it.'

'Well, well, I can see I've got an ace analyst in my squad. Very good, Jamie. I think you're absolutely on the ball. Our victories over Dinthorpe and Hemswell seem to have inflated our egos. We're floating on air instead of keeping our feet on the ground. So we fall for sucker punches because we're not looking out for them, not looking even where we're going. Then, when we lose, we feel a bit sick, or even, maybe, we sulk. Good analysis, son, good analysis. I can see you're in line for a coach's job yourself one of these days.'

Jamie made no answer to all that. Such flattery wasn't really Fixby's style at all. It didn't exactly sound like sarcasm but Jamie was sure that was what it was. In a moment the Boss would display his true feelings.

'You're not saying much now, Jamie,' the coach prompted.

'What do you want me to say?'

'I want you to say, now, how you think you got on tonight. As you reminded me – as if I needed reminding – you weren't playing against Odlington. So you shouldn't have been feeling the effects of that defeat so acutely. Though, *of course*, I realize your feelings for the *team* are always deep and unswerving.'

'I was poor, very poor. Actually, if it had been a proper match, you could have said I played a stinker.'

'Well done!' Mr Fixby positively beamed. 'I'm very impressed that you're just as skilful at *self*-analysis. Well, self-observation, anyway. Now comes the crunch question: WHY were you so bad? Was it that you were just sharing the general defeatism or is there a more subtle reason? Such as lack of enthusiasm because you won't be playing in the next match, either?'

Jamie lifted a foot on to the bench on which he was sitting and clasped his hands round his knee. Then he lowered his chin to rest it on the kneecap.

'Nothing like that, Boss, I promise. Even though I'm banned from the next couple of matches I'm determined to get back into the side as soon as possible. So it'd be stupid of me to cheat in training, stupid.'

'Right, for the moment I'll accept that's your attitude. It makes sense. So what *is* the problem? I've got plenty on my plate at present, so one more won't make any difference, whatever it is.'

'I – I really don't know. I mean, I feel OK physically and I want to play at my best and . . . .'

73

'Oh, come on, Jamie, you can do better than that!' Jonathan Fixby was plainly exasperated. 'Look, I know you've been subdued whenever I've been around. Are you still worrying about what happened to the Dinthorpe player you kicked?'

Jamie nodded. 'I can't get it out of my mind. I try, but I can't. Even when I do manage to forget it something crops up to remind me, something somebody says about injuries that affect people's *lives*. You know, just casually, they say it, but I immediately think of Billy Howard and what I did to him.'

'You haven't been trying to see him, have you, to apologize or something like that? You know what I told you, to leave it alone. That's the best thing for all concerned.'

'I saw him this afternoon,' Jamie admitted in a low voice. 'By accident, if you see what I mean. He was in the town centre, Church Street, getting along on his crutches. I was just coming out of a shop where I buy a pop music magazine. Almost bumped into him. Bit of a graveyard joke that, isn't it?'

He paused but Mr Fixby didn't say anything. He simply waited for Jamie to continue. It was, he knew, better for the boy to tell the story entirely in his own words. That way, the emotions would be released.

'Funny thing was, he wasn't mad with me at all. I thought he'd want to kill me if he got the chance. But he said he just accepted it was one of those things, I hadn't *meant* to break his leg. Could even have been the other way round and I could have been the guy in plaster! I was a bit shaken, I must admit, Boss. I mean, he said he still had

74

a hell of a lot of pain and terrible itching and he's no idea when the plaster is to come off. We – we didn't talk about when he might, *if* he might, play soccer again.'

The coach stood up abruptly. Then, without saying anything for a lengthy interval, he walked round the changing-room in a complete circle. Jamie, wondering what was coming next, kept silent, too. Clearly Fixby was going to say something he considered important. He was thinking carefully how to express himself.

'Look, that was a mad, bad, wild, senseless kick and it broke a player's leg,' he began in a very deliberate manner. 'But it was just *one* kick, no more. It wasn't pre-meditated violence. It happened in the heat of the moment. As Billy Howard told you, it could just as easily have happened the other way round, with you being the victim. A football match is made up of a thousand kicks, maybe several thousand, I've never counted and I don't suppose anybody else has. So that kick has to be looked at in the context of the whole match – one kick among many, among thousands. Nobody else's leg was broken by the rest of the kicks, was it? Of course not. One kick often decides the outcome of a match – a tap-in goal, a penalty, a foul – but it's never the whole match, it is never *everything*. It's just a tiny part of a match and it's just a tiny part of your life and it's a part you have to learn to forget, Jamie.'

He looked directly at Jamie and now Jamie was staring back at him.

'Billy Howard has forgiven you for what happened – he's prepared to forget it,' Fixby added emphatically. 'You must do the same to yourself. For your own sake, for the team's sake. You must forgive yourself – and forget the incident. If you don't, you'll completely destroy your own confidence as a player, and you'll help to ruin the team you're playing for. Understand, Jamie?'

Jamie nodded. He felt he ought to say thank you but he suspected Jonathan Fixby might not want to hear those words. After all, he wanted to convert Jamie into a hard man: and a hard man wouldn't go around scattering gratitude.

'I'll remember, Boss. Honestly, I only want to do the best for the team. I want Denholm to get to the top.'

'Well, you'll help us all, and yourself, if you start being a bit tougher again. Playing *hard*, for the team and for yourself. You help nobody by pussy-footing around. Football's a man's game, not child's play. So play it like a man. You know something? Billy Howard may be out of action for a bit with a broken leg. But he's braver than you. *Braver*. Why? I'll tell you why: because *you* can't stand the sight of *his* pain. And that's rubbish – a rubbishy attitude to life. Billy's adjusted to the situation, you've just told me that yourself, so you've got to do likewise. And from *now on*. OK?'

'OK, Boss.'

Fixby was nodding reflectively, as if with satisfaction at what he'd just achieved. Now he was about to add what he believed would be the clinching point: something that Jamie wouldn't forget.

'As I've said, son, this is a hard game, so you've got to *be* as hard as the next guy. You must never be willing to come off second best, however badly things might be going. You've got to be every bit as hard as somebody like

76

Ian Pickering. Ian, you know, would kick lumps out of his own grandmother just to score a goal.'

Carefully, he watched Jamie's reaction to that, deliberately provocative, remark. For some time he'd been aware that Jamie was jealous of Ian's success as a goal-scorer. Jealousy could inspire some players or it could destroy them. In this instance, he thought there was a chance it might work in the team's favour – if only young Austerby could be made to think on the right lines.

Jamie, however, rather spoilt things by saying nothing and displaying very little reaction apart from a slight tightening of the lips. Still, it was obvious that he'd heard the words. It was to be hoped he'd remember them – and act on them.

'Well,' said Jonathan Fixby after giving out a fairly theatrical sigh, 'I hope we've cleared up one problem now I've had a chat with you. Just wish some of the others could be solved quickly. Do you happen to know where Steve was tonight? He is a mate of yours, I think.'

'Er, no, Boss, no idea. I mean, he doesn't tell me much these days.'

'Just tells his girl-friend, I suppose. He *has* got a girl, hasn't he? That's what my spies tell me, anyway.'

'Yes – yes, my dad saw him with a girl the other day when we thought he was at the dentist's. He should have been playing for the school then, too. But I – '

'So you *did* know!' Fixby said accusingly. 'So the rumours are right. Well, next time you know something that is going to affect *our* team, perhaps you'd be good enough to put me in the picture. If a player is more interested in seeing a girl than playing soccer for a good team then I want to know about it. It's your *duty* to consider the consequences for the team, not the – the shallow feelings of a so-called mate. Right, Jamie?'

Jamie nodded. Until a few seconds ago he'd never have believed he could be in trouble just because he didn't split on a pal! But Mr Fixby had a masterly touch when it came to injecting a sense of guilt into anyone's conscience.

'Well, if girls matter more than goals to that young man I reckon I'll have to find somebody else,' the coach said with a return to his more relaxed manner. 'Don't suppose there's anybody you could recommend, is there? A lad who *wants* to play and *can* play?'

To his surprise Jamie thought of someone immediately. He couldn't imagine why he hadn't mentioned him before, except that Fixby had never encouraged his players to act as talent-spotters. Usually, he liked to find his own recruits.

'There's a boy at my school, plays in the same team as me, the School's Second XI, called Kieran Mallaby. He's really very talented, terrific on the ball, loads of confidence every time he's in sight of goal.' Jamie paused, feeling that he was already over-selling his team-mate. But Fixby just waited as if aware that there was more to come. 'But he's an out-and-out striker, not a midfielder like Steve. I mean, I don't know if that's what you – we – need . . .'

Fixby held up his hand like a traffic policeman. 'No, no, don't back-track. He sounds like my sort of player. So tell him to come along to the next training session and I'll run the rule over him. If he wants to play for the Avengers, that is, and isn't tied up with anything else, or anybody

78

else. I've got to strengthen the squad, so another striker will be an asset. We've got something coming up soon and I hope you're going to be involved. Should be really worthwhile, but I can't give you any details yet. Right, Jamie, I think that's been a very useful chat. Cleared the air of one or two things. And if this Kieran is all you say he is, well. . . . So, on that happy note, I think we'll call it a day – or do I mean a night?'

It was one of his favourite expressions and nowadays no one even smiled when they heard it. Jamie was on the point of wishing the coach good-night when he remembered that he had something coming up, too.

'Oh, Boss, I was wondering: what do you think of me playing hockey this Saturday? Vicky – she's my sister – fixed it up without my knowing anything about it in advance. It's not going to be easy to back out of it without, well, letting her down. It's a mixed game, boys and girls in the same team. Bit of a laugh, really, I suppose. . . .'

He thought that Fixby looked a little doubtful, but all he said was: 'Have you played hockey before?'

'Well, a bit, Boss. Vicky's terrifically keen and we sometimes practise together at home. Oh, and I once played in a boys' team on holiday.'

'Can't see that it'll do any harm,' Fixby declared, heading for the door. 'In fact, it might be good for you now you're off soccer for a bit. So, Jamie, go and enjoy yourself. Lay into 'em and show 'em how it's done. Bully for you!'

Six

Vicky was delighted to be getting a lift to the hockey match because, as she reminded everyone several times, usually she had to go by bus to her matches.

Jamie was less impressed. He thought his father should have transported them in the new truck instead of the old family saloon.

'You should be thankful you're getting a free seat all the way from home to playing fields,' Vicky told him. 'I know I am. I'll be worn out by the end of the afternoon, you know. It's much more exhausting spectating than playing.'

David Austerby glanced at his daughter through the rear-view mirror.

'Are you sure you're going to be warm enough in that skirt, Vicky? It really is *very* short and as you won't be running about all the time – '

'Oh, don't be an old fuss-pot, Dad! It's only what I'm used to. And anyway, I will be running about, up and down the touchline, cheering Jamie on when he's launching another attack. And I am a reserve, you know, so I might even get on to the pitch. Hope so. Then I can demonstrate my amazing new skills at dribbling right through the opposition.'

Although he hadn't admitted it Jamie, too, was sorry that his sister wasn't playing. They might have formed an effective partnership on Ankerton's right wing. But, really, she was just too young and inexperienced to be selected except as an emergency. He was hardly more experienced but had the advantage of being male in a squad that was short of men.

Ankerton had been set up originally as a works side. When the firm went bankrupt the team had stayed together and remained in the League, but when players left for one reason or another they hadn't always been replaced. Thus Ankerton had declined and nowadays were in the lowest division of the League. They could invite unregistered guest players to turn out for them, and that was how Jamie got into the team. Earlier in the week he'd almost made up his mind to drop out. Apart from being sure that he wouldn't enjoy the experience, he had a great fear that he'd do something quite idiotic, with the result that everyone, umpires, other players and spectators alike, would laugh at him.

Predictably, Vicky was furious when he hinted he might change his mind.

'Oh, no you don't, Jamie! If you don't play, you'll let *me* down, as well as yourself. I've set this up entirely for you. So you *owe* it to me to play.'

He was also aware that his banishment from the Sunday League soccer fields had exasperated her. She thought it was feeble of him to get caught out in a foul that could carry such a penalty. Sometimes he failed to realize how ruthless Vicky could be in her attitudes towards sport. So, with the encouragement of Jonathan Fixby and at the insistence of his sister, he was playing.

'How good are Pinwherry supposed to be?' he asked, turning in his seat to face her as they arrived at the Jubilee Playing Fields.

'No idea,' was the cheerful and uninformative reply. 'Tracey, the captain, has a policy of taking each match as it comes – just like football club managers always say they do! So she doesn't bother finding out what the opposition's like until she meets them.'

'Oh, great! So they could be world-beaters for all we know?'

'Could be,' Vicky agreed nonchalantly, 'but *unlikely* to be. After all, they're in the same Division as us – Ankerton – so they can't be that terrific. Still, they are next to the top so I suppose they're not bad.'

One thing was certain: Pinwherry were a very muscular side. In their red tops and blue skirts the girls in the team appeared to be just as physically well-built as the men with, possibly, one exception, a honey-blonde who lined up on the left side of midfield. She was almost as slim as Vicky but taller and unsmiling. It occurred to Jamie at the outset that at least she'd be easier to get past when he managed to join in an attack.

Ankerton, in their gold and green colours, were led by the girl playing centre-forward. Tracey never lost her enthusiasm and optimism however often her team was defeated, and it was her style to do all in her power to encourage her players to show positive qualities.

'Great to have you with us, Jamie,' was her warm-as-afurnace greeting. 'From everything Vicky says, you're going to be a great asset to Ankerton. Hope you're going to enjoy the game and play for us as often as you can. We need a speedy, crafty lad on the wing.'

Jamie hadn't expected a welcome anything like that, in spite of Vicky's forecasts. It made him resolve to do his very best for the side and help them to win their first game for (he'd been told) eight weeks. He could understand Tracey's reference to pace and youth: the majority of the team appeared to be distinctly elderly by youth club standards.

The start was sensational. Ankerton were awarded a free hit because of dangerous play by one of Pinwherry's central defenders. Without a moment's delay, Tracey herself struck the ball fiercely to the right flank where Jamie was hovering in almost complete isolation. Everyone else had expected the ball to be pushed forward and so Jamie had no one ahead of him as he flicked the ball down the wing. After recent heavy rain the centre of the pitch and the goal-mouths were little better than gluepots: but the flanks were well-grassed and relatively smooth. Jamie was quite exhilarated to find how well he was controlling the little white ball and even a sudden lurching challenge from the honey-blonde didn't put him out of his stride.

Ankerton's other forwards had moved up with unfamiliar perception, almost as if they knew they were about to be involved in some dramatic action. Jamie moved sharply inside and then, in response to Tracey's frantic yelling, he sent the ball hurtling into the shooting circle. In spite of all their experience of playing together, and in spite of their athleticism, Pinwherry were slow to see the danger and react to it. Their defence was practically non-existent. Desperately the goalie charged off her line to cut out the centre that threatened her goal – and in doing so she collided heavily with a full-back rushing to help her out. As they both fell, Tracey adroitly collected the centre and smacked the ball into the back of the net.

Ankerton 1, Pinwherry 0.

It wasn't only the players on the pitch who celebrated. On the touchline Vicky was leaping up and down with as much exuberance as if she herself had scored the goal.

'Great play, Jamie, great play!' she was yelling. 'Keep it up!'

Because her team-mate had unfortunately sat on her when they both went down, the Pinwherry goalie needed treatment from her anxious coach. It was, it seemed, her right leg that was injured and the pain-killing spray was liberally applied while the rest of the red-shirted players muttered darkly about the unexpected threat posed by Ankerton's new-look attack. Unlike Tracey, the Pinwherry skipper had checked up on the opposition in advance and seen little to worry him. But then, Jamie Austerby, the speedy, curly-haired right-winger, had not been playing for Ankerton on that occasion. The skipper went across to tell Lisa, of the honey-coloured hair, to make sure Jamie was well marked for the rest of the game. Lisa, who relished the hard girl shadow role, nodded.

Yet, in their very first attack after the resumption, Ankerton's forwards again made impressive progress. Tracey, revelling in the conditions, skilfully scooped the ball over two opponents' sticks before passing to Jamie. He was unceremoniously stopped by Lisa. In hooking her stick round his at a crucial moment she conceded a free hit. To her, that mattered less than halting the momentum of Ankerton's assault.

Following his captain's example, Jamie took the hit swiftly and whacked the ball into the middle. Once again, Tracey got into a scoring position when the ball was flicked on to her. But her shot hit the foot of the post. Still in pain, the goalkeeper was hopping about in a helpless fashion as the ball rebounded almost along the goal-line. She thought it was going out of play, anyway.

Jamie, though, was rushing in to back up his fellow attackers. He sensed, rather than saw, that the ball was going to stick in the mud. As others hesitated, he pounced. With the very tip of his stick he poked the ball into the net past the now transfixed goalkeeper.

That second goal stunned almost everybody. For some moments hardly anyone moved. Then Pinwherry's captain began to berate the goalie, who immediately claimed that she'd been given no cover at all. Tracey too seemed temporarily speechless. But then she chased after Jamie and practically threw her arms round him. He felt quite embarrassed, though the thrill of scoring so quickly after helping to set up the first goal conquered that emotion.

The real ecstasy was being exhibited, again, by Vicky. No one who hadn't realized it before was left in any doubt that the goal-scorer was her brother. She too wanted to rush over and kiss him but she knew very well he wouldn't approve of that. Tracey was quite enough for him to have to cope with at present!

Pinwherry were hastily holding consultations among two or three groups of players while the goalie received further, and this time unnecessary, attention from the trainer. But that short delay allowed the team to recover their composure. They'd believed that Ankerton offered no threat at all to their progress up the League table. Although slack defensive work had contributed to the deficit, it couldn't be denied that Ankerton had taken their scoring chances well. The goals would inspire them. So, as the skipper put it fiercely to his players, 'We have a mountain to climb. But climb it we will. Get stuck in everywhere!'

Suddenly, it became a very noisy game. Players were calling to each other all the time. The Pinwherry captain was forever yelling instructions to Kerry and Wendy and Stevie. No one was allowed to settle at all and Ankerton found themselves under sustained pressure. They expected to have to defend after scoring twice: and defend was what they did.

No yells were directed at Lisa. The skipper had already told her what was needed and she stuck like a limpet to Jamie, now regarded as Ankerton's real danger man. Tracey, too, was well marked and, by some luck and lots of endeavour, Pinwherry contrived to keep the ball away from the goal-scorers. Play was becoming increasingly physical, and the clash and clatter of sticks, punctuated by curses or cries for support, created something of a cacophony.

Twice Jamie tangled with Lisa and each time he was unable to win the ball. She was a skilful as well as an aggressive player. But it was the dirtier tricks in her armoury that worried him. The sudden, sharp push with one hand to send him off balance ... the flick with the stick that was aimed at his ankle, not the ball ... and, once, very painfully, the totally unexpected jab with the handle of her stick into his groin. That foul was committed when the ball had escaped both of them and the umpire was looking elsewhere. It was done so swiftly that even Vicky, following the play as intently as ever, didn't spot it.

Lisa, of course, didn't apologize. The expression on her pretty face didn't change. As, gaspingly, he recovered, Jamie himself might have imagined that it was an accidental collision if he hadn't distinctly felt her hand on the stick as she knocked into him. He determined to get his own back but couldn't think how he was going to do it. Players in a mixed match were supposed to be treated alike but he suspected that the umpire, a woman, might well act protectively towards any girl who was fouled by a male.

Jamie was dismayed. He and Vicky had played all manner of games for years, played hard and played to win: but never had they committed fouls against each other. It had never occurred to him before today that girls *would* play dirty, especially if they thought they could get away with it.

As Ankerton lost the initiative, so Pinwherry began to establish a rhythm in their play. Ankerton were being pushed further and further back as their opponents swept the ball laterally across the pitch and then attacked from new angles. Lisa hardly ever contributed to the game – except to maintain her attachment to Jamie. He was not the only one who was thankful when half-time was signalled.

'Phew! I thought we were going to give 'em a goal back

87

in that last attack,' Tracey remarked. 'I was glad when the whistle went, because they're definitely getting on top. But we held on well, men, we held on well!'

There was, indeed, a triumphant note in her voice. It was, as she said while sucking her half-orange, one of the fastest, most terrific games she'd played in for a long time. Definitely it was the best performance Ankerton had put up in months. If only they could hold on in the second half . . .

Before play resumed Jamie managed to get a quick, quiet word with her.

'Look, that girl marking me is a maniac, bashing me all over the place when she knows no one's looking. I mean, I'm not complaining, because I can take care of myself. But I might be able to, well, create more chances from the left wing. I play there at soccer so I'm used to it.'

Tracey nodded enthusiastically. 'Fine, fine, Jamie. Don't worry about Lisa, if she bashes you, bash her back. Girls get quite a lot of hammer from men, you know. This is a hard game. Or maybe she just fancies you! After all, you are a good-looking lad! Anyway, I'll get Bill to switch places with you. Actually, he prefers the right but I thought you should go there 'cos you're not as experienced at hockey and it can be awkward on the left.'

That ruse didn't work. As soon as Lisa spotted that he'd moved to the opposite flank she followed him and took up her gaoler role there. As before, she managed to avoid looking directly at him while making sure she missed nothing of what he was up to or planning. He was so annoyed by her presence that he completely missed his first opportunity to join in a movement, the ball running away under his raised stick for Lisa to sweep up efficiently. Tracey cast him a disappointed glance.

A minute later, in a hard-running, massed attack, Pinwherry forced the ball home to score their first goal – and give themselves hope that they could save this match. Simultaneously, Ankerton exhibited signs of apprehension about the outcome. Jamie felt doubly guilty about his own error of judgment.

Next time he saw a chance of gathering the ball he dashed towards it. His speed off the mark took Lisa by surprise. But she knew he'd have to slow down if he gained possession. Which he did, driving into a mêlée by the centre line and emerging unscathed. Lisa, cleverly darting behind two of her team-mates and using them as a screen, went headlong for her favourite victim. Because he had feinted to outwit another opponent Jamie was completely unaware of her approach.

He didn't even see her raised stick before it cracked him, precisely and viciously, on the ankle-bone.

The umpire had seen nothing of Lisa's assault. As Jamie fell, she skilfully collected the ball and sped towards the opposite flank to launch an attack of her own. When she parted with the ball the pass was beautifully weighted. Moments later Pinwherry's centre-forward calmly controlled the ball in the shooting circle and then fired it home under the goalkeeper's despairing lunge.

'The pain's absolutely *terrible*,' Jamie told Vicky when she reached him and tried to help him to his feet.

She didn't doubt it. She'd seen the tears in his eyes. What's more, she saw that, by sheer bad luck, it was the same ankle that was damaged in the orchard before the Dinthorpe match. And that injury was bad enough.

Tracey gave them a shrug of sympathy mixed with anguish. Knocks at hockey were commonplace and players usually got over them pretty quickly. She felt that Ankerton had suffered a worse blow in losing their lead. Now it would be doubly difficult for them to get back into this match. Pinwherry weren't the sort of team to be satisfied now they'd drawn level. They'd be going all out for the winner, and Tracey knew her own team weren't experienced enough to know how to cope with them.

As soon as he was off the pitch Jamie lay flat on his back on the grass while Vicky knelt at his feet and, removing his sock, applied the pain-killing spray she'd borrowed from Pinwherry's coach. She wanted ice but none was available. He'd have to wait until they got home for that. The coach was reluctant to surrender one of her rolls of strapping, but Vicky's prolonged pleading paid off in the end. Deftly, Vicky then strapped the ankle and persuaded Jamie to try to stand up. She knew he would claim that he couldn't.

'Come on, Jamie,' she added cheerfully. 'After all, the worst is definitely over now.'

'How do you make that out?'

'Because you know everything happens in threes, and this is your third injury – all in roughly the same region, oddly enough. So, after this, you shouldn't get another knock of any sort for, oh, I don't know, *months* I suppose.'

'I wouldn't bet on it with my sort of luck,' Jamie remarked gloomily.

Vicky listened to him resignedly. She didn't say a word about her own disappointment that she hadn't been called on as substitute to replace Jamie. Instead, Tracey had signalled for Sara, the other available substitute, to replace him. Sara was a solidly-built defender who wouldn't be intimidated by a runaway truck.

Together they watched the final minutes of the match. In spite of conceding two penalty corners in less than half a minute Ankerton somehow survived. They defended as if they knew a life would be sacrificed should they fail.

'Thanks for turning out for us, Jamie, and playing like a hero,' Tracey said as the rest of them strolled, and he hobbled, towards the bus stop. 'If you're fit again, we'd love to have you in the team again next week.'

'The way I feel now, I won't be fit for *anything* for months,' he replied.

Seven

Almost a week later Jamie was devotedly studying his ankle in his bedroom before getting down to some academic studies: history homework. That afternoon he'd taken part in a compulsory cross-country run and he still wasn't sure what the effect had been on his injured limb. Oddly, it hadn't pained him nearly as much as he'd expected. It was still discoloured, and a little puffy when he prodded it, but he had to admit it was recovering well. At this rate he might be able to contemplate soccer training the following week. His career as a hockey player had definitely ended, he'd decided.

Without warning, the door opened and Vicky sauntered in.

'Look, Vic*toria*,' he exploded, struggling to put his sock on at high speed, 'I've told you before, told you *millions* of times, I'm entitled to complete privacy in my own bedroom! You are not, repeat NOT, to walk in here without knocking – knocking *first* and then waiting to see if it's OK for you to come in. You know I never – '

'That ankle *must* be better by now after all I did to – to repair it,' she observed, ignoring his outburst as usual. 'From what I can see, it looks *tons* better. Good as new,

92

really. Sure you aren't *malingering*? According to the book I'm reading, that's what cowardly soldiers are supposed to do, the ones who can't face going into battle again.'

'It *feels* worse than it looks . . .'

'Rubbish! If the colour has faded, so has the pain. Anyway, Jamie, you can't malinger now, you've got to hop about a bit – downstairs, to start with.'

She paused, sank on to his bed and then said, with studied nonchalance: 'You've got a visitor. *Very* interesting.'

'A visitor? For me? Who is he?'

'How do you know it *is* a he? After the way you were such a hit with Tracey, to say nothing of Lisa, who was definitely a *hit* with you! I mean – '

'Oh come ON, Vicky! Is it a girl?'

'Why don't you go and see? This special person awaits you in the sitting-room. Getting a bit impatient by now, I shouldn't wonder, the way you're just malingering up here. . . .'

She just managed to escape from the room before he could grab her. Then, hastily, he combed his hair and checked the rest of his appearance in the mirror. As he went down the stairs he just had time to wonder why he was acting like this: after all, there was no girl he wanted to see or could imagine wanting to visit him. Still . . .

His visitor was Steve Derome.

'Hi,' he greeted Jamie, turning away from contemplating an aerial photograph of a Grand Prix motor-racing circuit that was on the wall above the television set. 'How's the old injury?'

93

'Not bad, not bad. But you asked me that at school this afternoon. . . .'

Jamie was utterly astonished to find Steve waiting for him. He wasn't sure whether he was also disappointed that it wasn't someone else.

'Oh yeah, so I did,' Steve agreed, 'but I sort of thought it might have changed since then, you know. The state of your precious ankle, I mean.'

It was plain he was nervous and not at all his usual self. He looked round as if expecting to see someone else in the room.

'Er, Jamie, do you think we'll be private enough in here? You know, no risk of interruption?'

'Depends whether Vicky zooms in. She's pretty unpredictable at the best of times.'

'*Pretty*, yeah, she is. Definitely. Bit young for me, of course. Has she got a boy-friend?'

'Not the faintest. I've no idea what she gets up to on her own.'

'You're not interested in girls, though, are you?'

'Sisters aren't girls! They're – just – girls.'

'I didn't mean that – but, oh well, skip it. I didn't come to talk about girls – well, not really. Money, that's what I wanted to see you about, Jamie old mate. Sorry to bring it up again. But could you possibly lend me a few quid? Things are a bit desperate at the moment, you see.'

Steve had been walking round the room, peering at various objects, as he spoke. Now he had come to a full stop and was looking his friend straight in the eye. When he used the word 'desperate' Jamie didn't for a moment doubt that it was accurate. Steve had never pleaded like this before.

Jamie didn't hesitate more than a few seconds before deciding what to do.

'OK, then, I can lend you something this time. Doesn't look like the group I was trying to form is going to get off the ground for a bit yet. So you might as well have some of the money I've been saving for that.'

Steve looked startled as well as grateful.

'Hey, you're a pal, a *real* pal! Thanks a million, Jamie. Honestly, I knew you wouldn't let me down. How much . . . er . . . can you manage?'

'Will a tenner do? I think – '

'Could you possibly stretch it to fifteen, Jamie? I mean, I know it's a terrific amount but . . . well, if you could.'

For a few moments Jamie didn't reply. Something had occurred to him, something he should have thought of before, but hadn't. Now, even before he asked the next question, he knew what the answer would be.

'You want this money for a girl, don't you? To spend on or to lend or something like that? That girl with copper-coloured hair, masses of it.'

This time Steve simply looked astonished.

'You've seen us *together*? But you can't have, we've been so – so careful. Melanie, especially, doesn't want anybody to know – even to *suspect*. It'd cause, well, all kinds of problems. Jamie, *have* you seen us together?'

Jamie shook his head. 'No, it was my dad. He spotted you in town one day when he was stopped at traffic lights. It was the day of the school match against Quarrington.

You were supposed to have a dental appointment, remember?'

Steve appeared marginally relieved by this news.

'Glad it wasn't anybody else who saw us. Fact is, it was Melanie who had to go to the dentist's. I just sneaked off so I could be with her. She needed – '

'You sneaked off from a *soccer* match to go out with a girl! You must be out of your mind. No girl's worth that.'

'Melanie is!' Steve replied spiritedly. 'She's fantastic. That's why I want to get her something really special for her birthday. There's some boots she's set her heart on. I want to get them for her.'

'Boots? What, sports *boots*?'

'No, you nut! Trouble is with you, Jamie, you've got a one-track mind. No, *fashion* boots, red-and-silver. They're quite nice, actually. I really admire Melanie's taste.'

Jamie wrinkled his nose and turned away. It was a movement which alarmed Steve.

'Jamie, you *are* going to lend me the money, aren't you? I mean, if I can't get these boots for her birthday she'll probably think I don't care for her, that I don't do what I say I'll do. I've said – I've said she'll definitely be walking out in those boots on her birthday.' He paused and then appeared to reach a conclusion. 'You see, Jamie, if I don't get them for her, somebody else *might*. Do you – do you know what I mean?'

Jamie shook his head again. 'Not really, no. But that doesn't make any difference, anyway. I promised, so I'll get you the money. You'll have to hang on a minute while I go and get it from my bedroom.'

He hurried upstairs and gathered fifteen pounds from the locked tin cash box he kept at the top of his wardrobe. It was perfectly obvious that Steve had called solely to borrow money: there was no sporting, or even social, reason for his visit. Jamie would be glad to see him go. At least he could then get on with his homework.

However, as soon as he'd stuffed the money into his back pocket, Steve seemed to feel the need to explain further about his relationship with Melanie.

'She's very popular, you know. Lots of other guys dating her – well, trying to! I mean, I'm the one she *really* goes for. There's a lad called Ricky who fancies his chances but he can't compete with me. Especially when she has those boots on her feet. And especially when she goes all the way to Finmere to watch me playing for Avengers in that tournament. I mean, that will prove to *everyone* that I'm the one she wants to be with.'

It wasn't until he saw Jamie's eyes narrowing that he realized he'd said the wrong thing. So he could guess what the question would be even before Jamie opened his mouth.

'What tournament are you talking about?'

Steve shrugged, half in embarrassment, half to dismiss the question as of little importance.

'Oh, something the Fixer's fixed up for that free weekend next month. I was thinking you knew all about it, of course. Sorry. But then, you weren't at training on Tuesday night, were you?'

'Not much point, was there? I mean, the ankle was still really painful then. I'd just have been a liability – Jonathan Fixby knows that.'

97

Again, Steve shrugged.

'Yeah, maybe, Jamie, but I reckon it's always best to keep in touch. Never know what might be going on that you ought to hear about. Anyway, I'm sure the Fixer'll be telling you all about it next time he sees you.'

Jamie was pondering.

'But if things are all definite, why didn't he phone me or – well, call in? He knows where I live – he's been here before. Did he say who was going?'

'Not exactly, no. We all just assumed that we're in the party because he didn't say otherwise. I mean, if you weren't being considered, Jamie, I'm sure he'd have told you by now. We all know he's a great one for the frank speaking – the bluntness of truth, as he puts it.'

Jamie didn't think there was much comfort to be derived from the fact that Jonathan Fixby had not contacted him. The coach could simply be waiting for an opportune moment when he next saw Jamie. Or he might even have thought he, Jamie, would be aware that he wasn't under consideration for a place in the team in the foreseeable future. That, as Jamie realized with a leaden heart, was a distinct possibility. It couldn't be denied that he was out of favour at present.

'Anything else special happen on Tuesday?' he wanted to know, wishing he'd been there so he did not have to ask the question.

'Not really. Oh – except that Kieran Mallaby turned up. He and the Fixer seemed to get on pretty well, from what I could see and hear.'

It was the final blow. He had, he sensed, suggested his own replacement.

He was scarcely aware that Steve was thanking him again for the loan of the money and edging away towards the door, murmuring that he had a date with Melanie and daren't be late for that.

Even though he spent the rest of the evening on his own, Jamie didn't manage to finish his homework.

Eight

The beginning of the end of Jamie's anguish came with a phone call the following Tuesday evening soon after he'd finished tea. As it happened, he was the nearest person to the phone when it rang, so he picked up the receiver: and was taken aback to hear Jonathan Fixby's voice.

'You are coming down here for training tonight, aren't you, Jamie?' he inquired in a mild, courteous tone.

'Well, er, I er, didn't know whether you'd, er, want me.'

'Of *course* I want you. You're part of my team, Jamie, so get down here as fast as you can. I mean, you are fit, aren't you? You haven't damaged any more ankles or knocked off any kneecaps?'

'No, no, I'm fine, Boss. Completely recovered.'

'Good. In that case, I'll expect to see you in double-quick time. We've got plenty of planning to do and I want everybody here who should be here.'

The receiver went down without another word being spoken. Jamie expelled breath in a long whistle. The coach had been amazingly friendly, considering that Jamie hadn't turned up for the previous Sunday's match and obviously hadn't been intending to train that evening. Jamie might well have expected a ferocious blast of anger when the next they met. Yet Fixby had taken the trouble to phone him and make welcoming sounds.

His luck was in again when he discovered that his father was going into town to play in a snooker tournament at his club and therefore could give Jamie a lift.

'You seem a heck of a lot chirpier tonight,' David Austerby remarked as he braked to a halt near the training ground. 'You seem to have been down in the dumps – or is it called the pits now? – for ages. I know you've had a lot of knocks lately but usually you shake them off pretty quickly.'

'Expect I was missing my football, Dad. You know, my *involvement* with the team. But it was my own fault. I was the one who decided to give it a miss for a bit.'

'Well, go and enjoy yourself, Jamie, and that'll make up for lost time,' his father said as he engaged gear and drove off.

'Hope you win *your* match!' Jamie shouted after him but didn't suppose he'd be heard.

He was the last of the squad to arrive. Because word had already circulated about his misfortune at mixed hockey there were a few jokes about his getting knocked about by a girl, but nothing that was really wounding. He knew he'd just have to laugh it off and agree with those who suggested he needed to toughen himself up for play-ing a man's game. Kieran Mallaby was present and already seemed to have slotted neatly and effectively into the Avengers' attacking formation. The big surprise to Jamie was the absence of Steve Derome, but nobody was referring to that. When Jamie tried to raise the matter with John Blakiston, the tall centre-back just shrugged and said he really knew nothing about it.

On the pitch the concentration was again on tactical ploys at set pieces. This time Jonathan Fixby wanted a more positive approach to attacking when the team gained a corner.

'We're just not getting into scoring positions at a time when the opposition is bound to be unsettled,' he declared, twirling his black and white scarf to give extra emphasis to his words. 'We've got to vary our tactics and make sure their defenders don't know what we're going to try next.'

'That shouldn't be difficult, because we don't know ourselves!' cracked Stuart Elcro.

The coach glared at him but didn't issue a reprimand. After all, it wasn't a bad joke.

'Speak for yourself,' John retaliated in his stead. 'You're always in a stew, Stu, so you can't be expected to know what's going on *anywhere*!'

Their cross-talk enlivened the training session and John showed himself to be in excellent football form by heading the ball into the net twice. On each occasion he was converting a corner kick that had been back-headed into the middle from Kieran Mallaby, stationed by the near post for that very trick. It came off extraordinarily well in spite of the fact that the defenders, both regular and makeshift, knew what to expect. Jamie was entrusted with several kicks, some taken with the left foot, others with the right, and he was delighted to discover that he hadn't lost his touch in any way at all. In fact, he'd rarely achieved such accuracy with his flag kicks.

Before the squad rounded off the session with a highly competitive, no-holds-barred six-a-side match, they practised taking short corners and here Kieran's skill on the ball when taking on defenders in and around the box drew exceptional praise from the coach. Jamie couldn't help having mixed feelings about Kieran's successful introduction to the squad. Inevitably, though, that was no more than Kieran himself expected. His self-confidence was rarely dented.

When they all returned to the changing-rooms the talk was about the tournament at Finmere, a small fishing port, nowadays better known as a holiday resort, on the east coast. John had once been there for a Bank Holiday week-end and he was enthusiastic about the setting as well as the amenities.

'Terrific cliffs at one end of the bay – near where we'll be staying. Be a great place to do hang-gliding, if you'd got the nerve.'

'You haven't even got the nerve to jump into a full swimming pool!' Stuart told him, and then ducked away from John's half-seriously sweeping fist.

'I'll dive deeper than you any day,' John promised. 'You can't even dive properly off your goal-line!'

There was no doubting the eagerness of everyone to enjoy the break from routine matches and ordinary home life at Finmere. Jonathan Fixby, naturally, gave the impression that he was more concerned with winning a trophy than having a good time.

'Don't forget, they'll be handing out medals to the winners,' he pointed out. 'So it's a great chance for us all to collect something, a souvenir of success, if you like. We're

103

not going to win our own League or Cup this season, unless a miracle happens. So don't miss out on this opportunity for a prize. We've got the players and I believe we've got the spirit to do well. But we've got to be professional in our approach. We've got to do the right things in the right way. Our behaviour and our attitude have got to be spot on. I know all of you are looking forward to this trip and the tournament. Well, let me tell you this: so am I. So, boys, don't let *me* down whatever else you do.'

He paused for that vital message to sink in. Then he looked round the room, focusing on every face in turn, but no one made any verbal response, not even John, the skipper.

'OK, then, that's it for tonight,' he concluded. 'But I want a word with you, Jamie, so I'd be glad if you'd stay behind.'

That unexpected request had the effect of reviving Jamie's worst fears. This 'word' from Jonathan Fixby was going to be an executioner's bullet: it would kill off his hopes of getting back into the team and enjoying the success and camaraderie of the squad at Finmere. Guy Kelton, his chief rival for a place in the side, would be there. So would Ian Pickering and Kieran Mallaby. Everyone would be there: except Jamie Austerby. He barely responded to one of the 'good-nights' from the rest of the players as they drifted away.

'Well, what're you looking so miserable about?' asked the coach, coming to sit beside him after a last word with someone else. 'You're fit again and, I thought, in pretty good nick on the pitch tonight.'

Jamie shrugged. He felt there was nothing he could say that would sound sensible.

'Problem is, *I* think,' Fixby resumed in a serious vein, 'that you're not totally committed – not totally committed either to Denholm Avengers or to soccer in general. You don't *care* enough. That's why you've skipped training and attending our matches when you weren't able to play because of the ban you received.'

'That's not true!' Jamie burst out. 'I *am* committed to soccer, honestly. I want to do well. I want my place in the team. But – well, I've been going through a hard time lately, haven't I? I mean, with all these injuries and then getting sent off and banned – and dropped even before that. That match against Dinthorpe when it all went wrong – I wasn't even playing at the start, was I? You'd dropped me down to sub. Nothing's gone right since then.'

'Stop feeling sorry for yourself, Jamie. That's always the easy way out – and it's the weakest thing you can do. Look, we all go through bad patches – can't escape them. They're part of life, if you like. The thing is to get over them as fast as possible. Put them behind us – forget them.

'Try and remember this: it's a privilege to be young, fit and talented – and you're all of those. You've got heaps of things going for you. If you weren't a talented player I wouldn't bother about you. But you have the skills I need for my team. That's why you're in the squad. It's your *attitude* that *matters* to me.'

Fixby took a deep breath and seemed to hesitate. Jamie sensed, though, that he should stay silent: that he shouldn't interrupt.

'Your attitude, that's what counts at the end of the day,

and at the beginning of the day,' Fixby began again, his voice lower and urgent. 'If you don't think – eat – feel – live – breathe football every minute of the day, every day of the week, then you're – an IMPOSTOR!'

He actually shouted the last word, to Jamie's discomfort and amazement.

'I don't think you are an impostor, Jamie, I think you're an intelligent and sensitive lad. Your reaction to the Billy Howard trouble shows that. But you have got to be a bit tougher, for your own sake. And for mine.'

Jamie nodded. He knew all that was true. What he hadn't realized was that Fixby had such a high opinion of him. Suddenly he felt flattered and eager to prove that the opinion was deserved.

'Thanks, Boss. I promise you – I won't let you down again. I'll give all the commitment you want. Honestly.'

'Good, good, because we're going to need the best from everybody at Finmere. Like I said, I want to come back from there as a winner.'

'I am in the squad, then, for Finmere? I mean, I didn't know what – '

'Of *course* you're going to Finmere! You wouldn't have been here tonight if I hadn't wanted you in the team for the tournament. I need the best and most committed players I've got. I'm relying on you making a great contribution, Jamie. You already have in another way – you put me in touch with Kieran Mallaby and I reckon he's going to add considerably to the strength of the squad. Good player – and a good attitude to the game. Just what we want.'

Jamie grinned. He felt as if the pain in a bad tooth had suddenly stopped throbbing. The world was bright again.

'But what about Steve Derome?' he asked. 'You said earlier about everybody being here who should be here and, well, Steve is missing and so – '

'Exactly! Steve is missing and he'll stay missing as far as I'm concerned. I go on about commitment because it's important, *vital*. And it's something Steve doesn't have any more. Steve can't be relied on. He's putting girls before goals – and when I say goals I don't just mean putting the ball in the net, I mean goals in terms of ambitions. So far as I can see Steve has no ambitions at present about soccer.'

The coach paused again for another of his clinching comments.

'That attitude's no good to me, Jamie son. I know Steve's a mate of yours but he's no longer a mate of mine in playing terms. You know what they say: no player's indispensable. Well, that's perfectly correct – and I've dispensed with the services of Steve Derome.'

Jamie, as he made his way home a few minutes later, could only feel thankful that a similar fate hadn't befallen him. It had, though, been a close thing. And that thought added to his determination to achieve success at Finmere.

Nine

Stuart Elcro was the one who insisted that they all went up on to the headland. He'd seen the cliffs on the opposite side of the bay as the train sauntered into Finmere earlier that afternoon. The railway line almost nudged the shore line and the view of the rest of the resort from the curving train was practically panoramic.

Denholm's goalie, true to form in his running rivalry with John Blakiston, had disputed that the cliffs were as spectacular as John claimed.

'The only way to prove it is to look down from the top,' John retorted. 'If you've got the nerve, that is, Green-shirt!'

That was a name Stuart detested. But he seemed unable to invent one that John resented. So he said no more until they booked into the sports complex where they, in company with three other teams, were staying for the duration of the soccer tournament. The general opinion was that the rooms were a million miles from the luxury class but the sports facilities were wonderful. If they had time they could swim, take a sauna, play squash, table tennis, badminton, hockey, rugby or even lacrosse. Soccer, of course, they would play. Judgement on the food would be made at

6.30 when the evening meal was served. Meanwhile, Jonathan Fixby had no objection to a group of his players taking a stroll from the sports complex to the headland. The sea breezes, he agreed, would be invigorating and therefore good for them after a long train journey.

Because he had not thought about doing anything else, Jamie tagged along with John, Stuart and Kieran, who seemed to have won the approval of Denholm's skipper. John Blakiston liked players who laughed at his jokes; and for some reason, possibly because he was the newest member of the squad, Kieran appeared to appreciate John's humour. Kieran carried an old tennis ball with him everywhere and so they played with it as they crossed the various sports pitches, an unfenced tarmac road bordering the complex and then the broad expanse of springy turf that stretched to the edge of the cliff.

Mostly they dribbled with the ball or kicked it at Stuart, who had invented the role of the non-stop running one-handed catcher. Whenever they allowed him to have the ball he showed he was in remarkably good form, whichever hand he used.

They had been passing through a wide hollow and the ground ahead of them sloped upwards to a crest on the distant skyline. As three of them exchanged passes two small girls trying to fly a kite darted between them. Only half-jokingly, Stuart made a grab at the low-flying, red, blue and white kite. But a sudden gust of wind lifted it well beyond his reach.

'Wendy, come on, before they try another snatch!' the chubbier girl with a pony-tail called anxiously to her companion.

Wendy's short hair and elfin features reminded Jamie of his sister.

Whooping joyfully after getting clear of the boys, the girls raced ahead.

'Another one you couldn't stop – and that kite's ten times the size of a football,' John chortled.

'Didn't need to,' Stuart replied airily. 'Going way over the bar, that one, wasn't it? Anyway, I don't need to impress *girls* with my skills.'

'Pity Steve Derome doesn't have the same attitude,' John remarked casually. 'Then they might like him a bit better. I mean, it's useless if you've got to spend *all* your time and *all* your money trying to impress a girl. Girls fall for the take it or leave it type. I should know!'

'But I thought Steve *was* having a great success with this girl Melanie,' said Jamie, puzzled. 'I thought that was why Jonathan Fixby rejected him.'

John laughed. 'Steve's chasing hard all right, but he's getting nowhere with old ginger-locks Melanie. She's got another lad she's really keen on. But Steve won't give up. He lavishes presents on her and pays the lot whenever they have a sort of date. He goes mad trying to think of things to do to impress her. But she's just stringing him along. And he's losing out on his football, all because of her. The Fixer won't let him back into the squad until Steve's madness is over – that's what Fixby calls, it, his madness. Dead right, too.'

'Oh, I see,' said Jamie, quietly. And he did see.

Kieran, fed up with all the talk about something he wasn't the slightest bit interested in, set off with the ball on his own to indulge in figure-of-eight dribbles.

'Come on!' John called to Jamie, now seemingly lost in his own thoughts. 'We'll both tackle him! Good practice for you.'

But before they could get anywhere near Kieran the girl with the pony-tail suddenly appeared at the top of the slope and then came hurtling towards them.

'Help me, help me!' she was yelling. 'It's Wendy, it's Wendy, my friend. She's gone over the cliff! Oh help me!'

Her distress made it obvious that she wasn't playing some sort of joke on them; she wasn't crying, but her eyes looked huge and haunted in a face that was as white as paper.

'What, right over the cliff? You mean, all the way down?' asked Stuart in disbelief.

'I don't know how far she's gone. She was on the edge where it slopes a bit. Then she sort of jumped up because the kite tugged at her. Then she fell over, slid on her side and – and – and *disappeared*.'

They all raced to the spot where it had happened. There the ground sloped quite sharply towards the edge for a distance of about eight or nine metres; and the grass, because it wasn't regularly trampled on, was longer and tufty. It was easy to see how the accident could have happened, because the dip in the ground was really like a slide – a slide that ended where the cliff fell away out of sight. There was no railing or barrier of any kind along that part of the coast; instead, at frequent intervals there were signboards which warned: 'Danger: keep well away from the edge.' Local residents and holidaymakers familiar with Finmere Cliffs were used to taking precautions up there.

Stuart, looking awestruck, was the first to break the

silence as they stared at the place of disaster.

'What're we going to do?' he asked in a hushed, urgent tone.

'Have a look to see if she's stuck somewhere,' Jamie promptly answered.

Then he took two or three sideways steps down the 'slide' before dropping on his stomach and wriggling backwards towards the edge. He had taken action before anyone else moved.

'Careful, Jamie!' Kieran called unnecessarily.

Jamie inched towards the edge and then, as he felt his feet project into space, he turned until he was lying parallel with the edge and could peer down. His handholds were two large tufts of grass, and he tested them for their strength.

'Wendy,' he called loudly, 'Wendy, can you hear me? Give a yell if you can.'

He could hear the waves washing the beach far below and distant cries of excitement from frolicking holiday-makers. Hard as he tried, he couldn't see very far down the cliff from where he lay because of the angle of the slope immediately below his position.

Then, just as he was about to call again, he heard, very faintly, an answer.

'I'm here, I'm here. Please help me! I'm stuck on a little ledge but I can't hold on for long. Help me, please!'

Jamie's heart jumped. He experienced a sense of enormous relief that the girl hadn't plummeted to the bottom of the cliff. A fall like that would surely have killed her.

'She's stuck on the cliff!' he called urgently to the other boys. 'Go and call for help – dial 999. The police or the fire brigade or somebody will come and get us up. I'm going down to help Wendy to hold on.'

'No, no, you mustn't!' John tried to insist. 'You'll risk your own life, Jamie! You mustn't!'

'I know what I'm doing,' Jamie said with confidence he didn't really feel. 'Just get help for us both.'

'Kieran's already gone – went off like a flash of lightning,' John told him.

Jamie eased himself over the edge. He was thankful he was wearing trainers, because they would at least give him a good grip when he found toe-holds. He still couldn't see the girl and so had no idea how far down he'd have to go.

'I'm coming down to help you, Wendy,' he yelled. 'So hang on, hang on! Don't move, whatever you do.'

The tough grass soon gave way to earth and rock, and then it became easier to find something to grip hold of as he moved downwards. At intervals he continued to call out to the girl that he was on his way and would soon reach her. He knew he had to try to convince her that she was safe. Twice he heard her little voice assuring him that she was still there. She didn't repeat that she couldn't hold on for much longer and Jamie was thankful for that. All the time at the back of his mind was the thought that she might have seriously injured herself, perhaps even broken a leg or an ankle. That was another reason why he had to save her – because he was thinking of Billy Howard.

His right foot searched for a hold and couldn't find one. Then, without warning, he dislodged some loose stones which went tumbling loudly down the cliff face. His mouth had dried up.

113

'That rock nearly hit me!' Wendy wailed. 'I'm right under you now. Please be careful.'

'Sorry,' he called.

It seemed to him very strange that she could see him now but that he still hadn't caught a glimpse of her. He decided he would have to shift sideways, both to find new holds and to prevent any more scree from disturbing her. In any case, he wanted to arrive on the ledge beside her, not on top of her head.

'You still OK, Jamie?' John Blakiston called anxiously.

'Yeah, fine. Making good progress.'

He actually felt quite confident now, much to his own surprise: more confident than when he'd climbed a tree to rescue Vicky's cat. Perhaps, he rationalized, that was because he was going down, not up. And yet, if anything went wrong he'd fall much, much further than he would have done from the tree. But he wouldn't *allow* himself to fall: his job was to ensure that Wendy was rescued.

'Hang on, Wendy!' he yelled. 'I'm nearly there. I must be.'

'You are,' she told him, and he was astonished how close she sounded.

He decided to risk a look round, and down. At last, he caught sight of her, a couple of metres away to his left and hardly more than the same distance below him. Her arms were wrapped round a root that was growing out of the cliff face at an angle of about forty-five degrees.

'Hey, I can see you at last!' he told her, recognizing the importance of talking to bolster her nerve and her aching muscles. 'I'll be with you in no time, Wendy. Don't let go, whatever you do!'

114

Edging across towards her was the hardest manoeuvre he'd yet attempted. The swell of the rock face at that point was a considerable obstacle and it was several moments before he could find finger-holds. All the time he was conscious that Wendy's strength must be ebbing. The root to which she was clinging was above the level of her head, and so the strain on her arms would be enormous. It was just as well that she was slimly built and so must weigh very little.

A swooping seagull that came in very close, as if to investigate this strange creature invading its territory, suddenly let out a cry that almost unnerved Jamie, because he hadn't been aware of its presence.

Then, as he felt with his toe for a foothold, a piece of rock broke away under his shoe – and bounced noisily down the cliff. Jamie involuntarily let out a gasp.

'Stay still, stay still!' Wendy yelled at him. 'You're safe, don't worry.'

That was remarkable proof that she was far from losing her nerve. She was now trying to look after him!

'Thanks, Wendy. But I'm only resting a moment. Be across in a second.'

In fact, it took him five more minutes to reach her. He never doubted that he would get there, and stand on the tiny ledge beside her, but each move had to be calculated like moves on a chess-board.

'Right, you can relax now!' he exclaimed as he put one arm round her and, with the other hand, took a firm hold of the bush that had saved her. 'All we've got to do now is wait for someone to pick us up. One of my mates has gone for help. Should be back in no time.'

He saw that her eyes were glistening with tears of relief, but she managed not to cry. Now that he was so close to her it struck him again how much she resembled Vicky.

'Will they send a helicopter, do you think?' she asked as she flexed her fingers, stiff after clutching the root of the bush with such ferocity.

'Doubt it. We're not really that far down the cliff, are we, so I expect the police or fire brigade will just send down a rope to pull us up. Or maybe a net. They could throw that over us to prevent us falling in the excitement of being rescued!'

After yelling to John that he had reached Wendy and she was perfectly safe, he talked to her about her hobbies and her family and her friend, Emma, the girl with the pony-tail. It transpired that the kite was brand new; Emma had received it only the previous day as a birthday present.

'She was so scared of losing it. That's why I tried to save it from sailing over the cliff when she let go of it,' Wendy explained. 'Funny thing is, we both thought you and the other boys were going to snatch it from us and never give it back. And now – now you've risked your life to save me. I'll never forget you as long as I live, honest.'

Before Jamie could make any response to that declaration there was an excited yell from Stuart Elcro.

'They're here, Jamie, they're here! It's the fire brigade and they say they'll have you up, safe and sound, in a jiffy. So don't panic!'

Jamie managed a laugh at that. 'We haven't panicked so far, Wendy, so I don't think we will now, do you?'

'*You* haven't, anyway,' she told him. Then she asked his

name. When he told her she said: 'I think you're a hero, Jamie Austerby. And I've never met a real hero before.'

Then a voice boomed at them from a megaphone: 'Hello, Jamie and Wendy! This is the fire brigade here. One of our firemen is coming down on the rescue rope to collect you. Any moment now. He'll bring you up one at a time. So just stay as you are and leave the rest to us.'

Almost before that news had registered with them their rescuer was snaking down the cliff face on a line attached to the fire appliance parked on top of the cliff. He was a bulky figure with a comforting smile and a warm voice.

'Right, then, let's have you!' he announced as he swayed to a stop beside them. 'Ladies first, I think, so I'll take you up, Wendy, and then come back for you, son. OK?'

So Jamie released the girl into the fireman's embrace. After a signal on the rope they were hauled upwards with, to Jamie, astonishing speed. There was hardly time for Wendy to shout: 'See you, then, Jamie!' But she managed it before disappearing from his sight.

It seemed to be only moments before the fireman was returning to lift him, too, to safety. Jamie experienced an unexpected reaction when he stood again on firm ground with acres of space to move in: for a moment or two his legs began to tremble and he feared he might fall. (Later a doctor called to the sports complex to give him a check up explained that was quite normal: his muscles and his nerves were simply coming to terms with the tension they'd been experiencing during the ordeal on the cliff face.) What surprised him was the number of people already gathered there to greet him and Wendy: and there was a great burst of applause and clapping as the fireman and he shook hands.

Then Wendy, who appeared to have made an instantaneous recovery, rushed forward to put her arms around him and kiss him. Jamie thought that was just about the most embarrassing moment of the entire incident; but he didn't say so. He'd begun to admire Wendy's spirit.

Most of the Denholm squad, alerted to what was going on by the fleet-footed Kieran, were in the crowd of holidaymakers and onlookers and firemen. Now they surged forward to slap Jamie on the back and crack a few jokes. John Blakiston, inevitably, said that Jamie's save was better than anything Stuart Elcro would manage in a lifetime of goalkeeping! The one person who might have been there and wasn't was Emma: she had been so overcome by anxiety during Jamie's rescue bid that she'd been taken home to await news there. After all, at that stage, no one could be sure that Wendy and Jamie would be brought to safety.

It was Jonathan Fixby who drew Jamie aside from the public gaze for a word in private.

'That was tremendous, Jamie, tremendous!' he said with a fervour that Jamie had never heard from him before. 'Took real guts – and imagination – and nerve. I tell you, son, I'm really proud of you. We're *all* proud of you. You're an inspiration to the whole Avengers' squad. I shall be telling the Press that, you can be sure.'

'The Press?' Jamie was very surprised. 'But you don't have to tell them about what's happened, do you? I mean, if my parents read about it they might really worry and, well, want me to go back home to make sure I'm unharmed – and so on.'

Fixby was shaking his head.

'Couldn't be avoided even if I wanted to keep it secret, which I don't,' he said. 'Dramatic rescues like this are automatically reported – the fire brigade themselves have to be in touch with the papers about what they get up to each day. So are the coastguards, who would have been here to rescue you if they hadn't already been out on call further up the coast. Seems this is a busy day for the emergency services.'

He paused and gave Jamie a searching look. 'Anyway, the Press boys will be along later for a word and a picture. Your opportunity for a bit of fame, you see. Then you can ring your parents later to warn them what to look out for. I'll be on hand, anyway, to see that you're able to give a coherent account of events.'

Once again the coach paused. Then he resumed: 'How do you feel, Jamie? Inside, I mean. If all this terrific excitement gets on top of you I can let you have a sleeping pill or two. Always keep some handy for those players who get nervy the night before a big match. Best to be sure, because a good night's sleep is essential.'

'Oh, I feel fine, Boss, truly. Top of the world, really. Talking about tomorrow's match – er, will I definitely be in the team then?'

The coach's expression altered just a fraction; and there was a lighter tone to his voice.

'Oh, well, son, it's a bit too early to make decisions like that. We'll just have to see how you get on in the next few hours. So we'll review things in the morning. OK?'

There was nothing Jamie felt he could say in response to that.

Ten

Jamie enjoyed his breakfast. He still had no idea whether he was going to play for Avengers that day, because Jonathan Fixby wouldn't announce the line-up until he held his team talk at nine o'clock. But Jamie had given up worrying about whether he'd be selected. He was absolutely confident that even if he were 'rested' for the opening match of the tournament against Devoran Raiders he'd be in the side before long.

He sensed that things were going his way. For a start, he'd actually become quite famous, almost literally overnight. There were stories about him in several newspapers, including one under the headline: 'Boy soccer star in cliff rescue drama.' Of course, as his team-mates lost no time in pointing out, he wasn't a soccer star at all; but then the Press often exaggerated a few details to make a better story. He'd been photographed with a solemn-looking Wendy (she'd been asked to adopt a serious expression to underline the ordeal she'd been through) and received the heartfelt, and many times repeated, thanks of her parents. On the phone he'd talked to his own parents and Vicky and reassured them about his well-being; and they'd promised him a wonderful welcome-home party when the

tournament was over. After all the excitement of the previous evening he'd slept just as well as he always slept. As
soon as he awoke he felt, both mentally and physically, in
top form. There wasn't a trace of anxiety about anything
in his mind. The jokes by his team-mates about his 'hero'
status he fielded with complete nonchalance.

'Jamie, a word with you, now, please,' said Jonathan
Fixby, appearing unexpectedly in the doorway as a group
of Denholm players were on the point of leaving the
dining-hall.

For once the coach had discarded his duffle coat and his
ancient scarf; like every other team official Jamie had seen
so far, Fixby was wearing tracksuit and trainers. In any
case, there had been a distinct improvement in the
weather: it was a mild, spring-like day with a hint of sun
and warmth to come.

Jamie couldn't guess from the expression on the coach's
face what the word was going to be. Fixby led him to a
small office beside the changing-rooms. There, in casual
fashion, he dropped into a chair behind a desk bearing a
typewriter; Jamie because he hadn't been invited to sit in
the only other chair in the room, remained standing. But
for the presence of the typewriter he felt he could have
been facing an interview with a headmaster.

'So, how're you feeling today?' the coach wanted to
know.

'Fine, fine. Great, really. No problems.'

Fixby nodded. 'Thought so. You looked in pretty good
nick when I saw you kicking a ball about with some of the
other lads before breakfast. Sleep all right?'

'Definitely.'

Again Fixby nodded. 'Good. Well, it seems you're not suffering any adverse reaction to yesterday's high drama. Being a hero, as the Press describes you, obviously suits you, Jamie! Well, now I want you to be a hero for the Avengers today. Do you think you can cope with that as well?'

Jamie grinned. 'I'll do my best, Boss.'

'Yes, I'm sure of that, Jamie. I think that what happened yesterday could have been a great fillip for you. You demonstrated your quick thinking and you demonstrated your nerve. They paid off for you. Now I want you to demonstrate the same qualities for Denholm. I think you can do a great job for us. But one word of warning, Jamie.'

Predictably, in Jamie's eyes, the coach paused for greater emphasis. His style never varied.

'If things start to go wrong for you then I won't hesitate to pull you off. If you aren't contributing, if you start *hiding* from the ball instead of *demanding* it, then off you come, yesterday's hero or no yesterday's hero. Got it?'

'Yes, I've got it.'

'Good. Just one thing, Jamie. And remember it. If you *feel* like a winner, you *are* a winner.'

Jonathan Fixby said very much the same thing at the team meeting a few minutes later. Plainly it was his new slogan for success. Nobody wondered where he'd got it from; they simply expected him to come up with catch phrases that summed up a playing philosophy.

He emphasized, again as they all expected him to, that the tournament was there for the winning and he wanted Denholm to win it. They were capable of winning it, so

123

they *must* win it. Everyone was in the party on merit, so if they played at their best there was no other team to stop them. Certainly not Devoran, their first opponents . . .

Devoran Raiders were a Cornish side and, unluckily for them, they'd been held up on their long journey from the West Country by a faulty locomotive that expired completely in Exeter and so had to be replaced. So they were several hours late in reaching Finmere the previous evening.

'They're bound to be a bit jaded, so we've got to attack them right from the kick-off,' Fixby told his players in the changing-room a few minutes before the match began at 10.30. 'We must kill 'em off before they've had time to draw breath. Remember, *I* want to win this trophy, so *you* want to win this trophy.'

Then he picked their shirts off the pile beside him and hurled them, one by one, to the chosen eleven. Jamie couldn't help glancing across at Guy Kelton as the slimly-built winger tugged on the No. 12 shirt, the one Jamie himself had worn in that fatal match with Dinthorpe. The name of Billy Howard crossed his mind, but he didn't dwell on it. The Dinthorpe game, and all that went with it, now seemed a century ago.

The Cornish team were in an unusual strip of chocolate-brown-and-yellow and didn't appear at all exhausted. They were bouncing up and down and rapidly running through a variety of exercises before Denholm even got on to the pitch. Plainly they were every bit as eager as the Avengers to get on with the game.

Two other games were being played simultaneously on adjacent pitches, but the greatest number of spectators wanted to watch Avengers v Raiders, possibly because of their names but more probably because playing for Denholm was the 'boy soccer star' of popular Press fame. The local newspaper had sent along one of their photographers to get a shot of the new Finmere celebrity in action on the pitch less than twenty-four hours after risking his life on the cliffs.

Jamie wasn't slow in providing the cameraman with what he – and the spectators – wanted. From the kick-off Kieran, receiving the ball from Ian Pickering, kept it for only two strides before hitting it firmly to the left flank. In anticipation of that pre-arranged move Jamie, instantly into his stride, seized possession and rounded his first challenger with an ease that astonished every onlooker – and the challenger.

Cutting inside as soon as the next opponent loomed up, Jamie flicked the ball from one foot to the other and then, catching the Devoran player off-balance, veered out to the flank again. The pace of the move was bewildering the Cornishmen. Their defence didn't know whether to retreat or to try to dispossess Jamie by weight of numbers. He didn't give them a moment to try to make up their minds. With another change of direction, and then pace, he outwitted a third adversary and was in sight of the goal-line. Kieran was now heading towards him, calling for the ball; but only Jamie knew that was a ploy worked out between them. The Raiders hastily tried to attach an extra marker to Kieran, already rumoured throughout the Finmere sports complex to be an outstanding ball-player on the basis of the form he'd shown in training the previous evening.

Jamie's target was Ian's head. Glancing up, he saw that the tall striker was right on course for the penalty area – and because of Kieran's diversion was at present unmarked. As yet another challenge came in Jamie rolled the ball backward with the sole of his boot, tilted his body first one way, then another: and suddenly accelerated with the ball at his toes again. Now he had time: now he had space. All that was needed was accuracy as, almost from the goal-line, he swung the ball over into the middle.

Ian's timing was every bit as good as Jamie's. None of the opposition picked him up as he raced in to meet the cross – and the ball had been angled far enough back for the goalkeeper to be uncertain whether to stay on his line or come out. He dithered: and so was helpless as Ian jumped to head the ball firmly into the top right-hand corner of the net.

Denholm Avengers had taken the lead after only forty-four seconds – and before even one Devoran player had touched the ball.

'Great cross, Jamie, great cross!' Ian exulted as scorer and provider met in a dervish-like dance on the way back to the centre spot.

And it had been the perfect centre. Jamie had no doubts about that; this was not a moment for false modesty. He sensed before he even released the ball that it was going to lead to a goal. He sensed that his days in the wilderness were over. He was back on top form, eager for the ball and confident he could use it to maximum advantage. He glanced across to the touchline, where Jonathan Fixby was applauding enthusiastically. No coach could have wished for a better start by his team to a Cup tournament.

One certainty now was that Devoran Raiders would take a closer interest in the curly-haired winger with the deadly left foot. Jamie Austerby would be marked down as the danger man: and marked out of the rest of the game if possible. Unless the Cornish players were different from every other team he'd faced, Jamie knew that he'd become the target for some fierce, uncompromising tackling by their defenders. That thought didn't disturb him one iota. His ambition to outwit the opposition did not diminish.

Quite inevitably, the ball soon came his way again, pushed out to him by Kieran, who was equally keen to add to his reputation by forming a profitable partnership with a player obviously in form. This time Jamie deliberately took the ball up to a full-back to see what the reaction would be. The defender was as tall as Ian Pickering and, if anything, thinner. Initially he back-pedalled furiously – and then lunged forward like a striking snake. But Jamie anticipated that move – and flicked the ball sideways for Kieran to collect. That move led to nothing, but Jamie knew he would have no real trouble with that defender; his technique was unsophisticated and much too obvious.

Devoran recovered well from the initial setback. Their skipper was their chief striker and, although he did a lot of shouting, he led by example. In the fifth minute he set off on a Kieran-type solo run, rounding John Blakiston with alarming ease, and then fired only just over the bar from outside the box. John had been taking things too easily and he got a clenched fist sign from the coach.

Jamie continued to revel in his attacking role whenever the ball was switched in his direction: and when it wasn't coming his way he went in search of it. Physically, he felt to be in wonderful form; there was no worry in his mind about anything – apart from not getting enough of the ball! Several spectators cheered him on every time he had possession: but it was some minutes before he became aware that one of them was Wendy. She was with her parents and it was clear that he now had his own fan club. That didn't do his ego any harm at all.

'Go on, Jamie, give us a goal!' Wendy yelled at one point when she realized that he'd seen her.

Then, just as it seemed that Devoran were getting on top and threatening to equalize at any moment through the outstanding skills of their skipper, the second goal arrived. Once again, Jamie was involved, but he wasn't the scorer.

With less than a minute to go before half-time Ian Pickering was tripped crudely in the centre circle. Graham Aspinall, who played on the right side of midfield for Denholm, surprised the opposition by hitting the free kick right across the pitch to where Jamie was loitering on the touchline. He turned the ball inside and started to run. But although he had space ahead of him and no challenger, suddenly he struck the ball diagonally back into the middle of the pitch. Instinctively, he knew that was the sort of pass that Kieran wanted. He'd seen him make the most of such openings in school matches.

Kieran pounced on the ball like a cat on a mouse, feinted to go one way, ducked the other and then, with a nice change of pace, swept past his first opponent on his original route. Devoran's defence again retreated, expecting Kieran to steer the ball out to the wing again. Kieran had no such thought in his head. He was going for goal and no one was going to stop him. Ian Pickering was still recovering from his knock in the centre circle and so support was minimal. But Kieran simply showed that he didn't need it. With another devastating swerve he reached the penalty box. By now the goalie knew he had to come out and hope to smother the ball by flinging himself at Kieran's feet.

The striker guessed that would happen. And so he waited until the goalie dived. Whereupon he slid the ball under his opponent's body and all along the ground into the back of the empty net. By any reckoning, it was a brilliantly taken goal.

That goal couldn't have come at a better time, of course, and Jonathan Fixby said so to his players as they gathered round him during the interval. Devoran, he stressed, would come out fighting in the second half, totally determined to get back into the game. If they didn't score soon, the tournament might be as good as over for them. Remember, he reiterated as they went back on to the pitch, goal difference would count if points were level at the end of the first round of matches: so the Avengers should be striving to score as many goals as possible.

'Don't sit back on your lead,' were his final words.

There was no hope of being able to do that. Predictably the Cornishmen camped in Denholm's half from the restart and, within seconds, they had the ball in the net. The goal wasn't scored quite as fast as Ian's, which opened the first half, and it wasn't of anything like the same quality. Indeed, it was a scrambled affair, a toe-poke by Devoran's central defender following a complete mis-kick by John Blakiston, who should have cleared his lines moments earlier. But it counted. That was all that mattered to Devoran, because they knew that one more goal would put them on level terms. Then the match would be wide open. None of the Avengers dared look at Jonathan Fixby. They could imagine his reaction only too well.

All at once, the pace of the match became furious. No longer was anyone holding on to the ball and attempting dribbles or calculated passes. Everyone seemed anxious to get rid of the ball and boot it as far as possible. No one was going to be caught in possession. On the firm pitch the ball was bouncing high and where, in the first half, the ball-players had been in control of the situation, now they appeared incapable of dictating the play. The tempo didn't slacken as play rocketed from one end of the pitch to the other.

One player not greatly involved in the action was Jamie. Because of the change in tempo the ball was being hoofed down the middle of the park; no one was pushing it out to the flanks. Jamie, tired of waiting and eager to contribute something again, moved into the crowded midfield; but there, by one misfortune or another, the ball still eluded him. He began to despair of ever getting another touch, except by accident.

The minutes were ticking away and neither side could manage to combine effectively or make the vital breakthrough. Tension was high but, miraculously, tempers didn't fray. The spirit of the game couldn't have been bettered. For the umpteenth time Fixby looked at his watch and wished the referee would blow for time. Devoran were displaying no lack of stamina: their sleepless journey from the far west seemed not to have affected them at all.

Not a single player gave any hint of tiredness, let alone exhaustion. Now, as their defence re-grouped yet again to cope with a corner kick on the right, their skipper, who hadn't stopped talking for half a minute throughout the game, urged them to hold on, hold ON! By now the referee was looking at his watch, too.

Jamie edged in towards the far post. His marker, the tall full-back, kept him company. Kieran took the kick, floating it perfectly to the near post where John Blakiston had stationed himself for a back-header. John moved out a couple of paces and got to the ball first, to send it looping over his head into the centre of the penalty area for Ian to reach. But Ian, naturally, was well marked and couldn't make quite the contact he wanted. The ball spun off Ian's cheek, ricocheted from someone else's shoulder and then bounced awkwardly between two defenders who were obstructing their goalkeeper.

Jamie didn't hesitate for a fraction of a second. The instant he saw his chance he dived for it, throwing himself headlong at the ball as feet came up to kick it clear. But it was Jamie's forehead that made contact first. From an almost horizontal position he nudged the ball beyond the goalkeeper's despairing arms and into the net.

Someone tumbled over him as he got to his feet but he didn't give a thought to the bruises and the scratches. He had scored, he had restored Denholm's two-goal advantage in the dying moments of the game. Even as he hurled himself at the ball, without thought of the risks he was taking, he was certain he would get a goal.

His team-mates thumped him on the back and told him he was a hero all over again. Then, when the referee ended the game seconds later, Jonathan Fixby was the first to rush on to the field to congratulate him.

'I *felt* I was going to get the winner, so I got it!' Jamie told him with a victor's smile.

'That's just the way it should be, Jamie,' Jonathan Fixby responded. 'And because of what you've done, *I* feel we're going to win this tournament.'